BANK HOLIDAY HURRICANE

BANK HOLIDAY HURRICANE

Kelly Creighton

Doire Press

First published in 2017

Doire Press
Aille, Inverin
Co. Galway
www.doirepress.com

Layout & design: Lisa Frank
Cover photo: TomthePhotographer / unsplash.com
Author photo: Ryan Creighton

Printed by Clódóirí CL
Casla, Co. na Gaillimhe

ISBN 978-1-907682-54-4

We gratefully acknowledge the assistance of The Arts Council of Northern
Ireland.

LOTTERY FUNDED

CONTENTS

For Ryan

BANK HOLIDAY HURRICANE

Here are the lines you know and expect. Do what you must to stay between them.

L ife is long. When the sky falls, there is no point sitting under it, twiddling your thumbs. That's when it starts to nip at you. What you really need is to have a plan. Mine looked like this: *get an education, get the hell out of here.* It was hardly complicated.

I'd painted a picture in my mind of where I was going in the end. I spent years thinking. Nothing else for it but thinking. Being taught different ways to think. I kept busy on that Bachelors degree in Philosophy, and on top of that, the Masters in Eng. Lit. I had fourteen years wrapped up before long.

I was six years in when Ruth wanted a game of table tennis. We played for months. She said her friends would get her out, they set an appeal date and won. I should have been happy for her but I wasn't. Just before she left, I said I hoped Ruth would never get her kids back. She used to talk about them, how her youngest would be starting school the coming September, how the big one, the daughter, turned eight on the tenth of May. Every year since I've remembered that date.

After her release I had nothing to do with all Ruth's information so I didn't bother with anyone else. People swarmed the place, came and they left. I headed to the prison library when I could, found I no longer hated the texts they made us read back in school. Choice is everything. I held a copy of *Wuthering Heights* in my hands and wondered about myself changing like I had. I read lines that made me have to stop, to set the book down, still splayed open, because it felt like the full stops were eyes and every one could see right through.

On the outside I would have completed the course in much less time, but really it's not what I would have done on the outside at all. Picking life experiences up off the floor is what I would have been doing: like the day I went to choose a wedding dress, and I was keeping my mother back from something more pressing. She had a quare sourpuss on her, browbeat me into taking the first one I tried.

Moments like that one helped me understand characters' disappointments and hurt and disdain. How they had to let life disappoint because it is written like that.

To begin with I couldn't live with myself. I don't remember much but the waking up, warden over me massaging my heart. I learnt that was a figure of speech, there was nothing massaging about it. In the shower I saw the plum bruise between my breasts from the heels of his hands and in the mirror the blooming purple sausages from the ligature. I didn't feel alive but I no longer wanted to die. I can talk about it now.

I used to live in a dive of a place. I got out of there as soon as I could. Aidan was my way out. He asked me to move in when we'd been together two weeks. He told me he'd a spare room. Aidan also told me he had a job, a Sky box and a car. He let on he had a cooking qualification and talked up a good game of the meals he was going to rustle up for me. Rustle is an effortless word.

Aidan was a big lump of a lad. I said he looked like he enjoyed a good feed and he could cook me anything he wanted. I'll spoil you pure rotten, Aidan said. What are we waiting for then? I said.

Two weeks. There was no spare room. He couldn't cook for shit, sat on the sofa-bed all day watching episodes of *Top Gear* on video. Aidan asked if I'd like to put a new sofa in my name and I did. It was leather and soft as butter. He lay across it to watch *Top Gear.* Jeremy Clarkson was dark-haired and considerably less craggy then. My twelve-year old sister called him *a ride.* It made me laugh. Clarkson drove flash cars and pulled his jeans up to his nipples. Aidan wore his around his arse. He asked me if I thought Clarkson was a ride too. He asked me who did I think was?

Nobody, I said because those don't end well.

He nodded at his jacket that was hung on the door handle. The handle was broken. I don't think we knew things like that could be fixed. He put his hand in his pocket and took out an H. Samuels box, his face sort of melting.

It wasn't what you'd call a long engagement. Aidan didn't want a fuss, nor did he want a party. He said engagements were the scotch tape of broken couples. All he wanted was to be my husband, and he was. I dragged my mother away from her own TV set and tried the wedding dress on in front of her. She said it was good material, it had washed up like a ribbon. A pigeon flew straight against the charity shop window and lay on the ground wounded, one wing twitching like a tired eyelid. The charity shop woman was disgusted. You could see my mother was sickened too. I'd only known her to be squeamish about two things: dead birds, for that reason she had an unreasonable hatred of cats, the other thing was checking her breasts, following her one and only time she did, and found a benign cyst. Never again, she'd said.

My mother got out her credit card. Seventy pound, is it? she asked, and told the woman to bag the dress up.

Over there is a lovely gold one like in the magazine, I told her, but she was keying in her pin, glancing at the spot where the beak had scored the glass.

Not with your colouring, the woman said.

I thanked my mother for the dress. She could never handle a thank-you well. I told her I'd stay and look for shoes and a veil that I'd buy myself. She took the dress to her house. The next day I cried in the shower. That behaviour was becoming a fact of life.

My mother never told me who my father was. Les was my step-dad. When I was three, Les came on the scene, they met when they worked together in the bar. There was a robbery one night and they, with a customer, were kept hostage. In a spasm of bravery Les tried to wrestle the gun away and was shot in the arm. My mother brought Les to her house to look after him. My sister was born a year later.

My mother never loved Les. A bat could see that. My mother told me he used his bad arm as an excuse, he clocked all day, did nothing, had her ironing shirts and cleaning boots as if he had somewhere to wear them. She told me if it wasn't for the fact he didn't pester her for sex anymore, she wouldn't have been so tolerant of him. She told me, Marry a man you fancy the arse off.

I intend to, I said.

My mother kept working till I was sixteen then she told me to get out or get to work. Les told me I was welcome to stay as long as I wanted. It was big of him, I thought, considering. He started his weekends on a Tuesday lunch and drank himself sick by Saturday night. Aidan said he admired Les' commitment. We all used to meet up for dinner on a Sunday. My mother would take the Chinese take-away bag from me and plate up.

It made me ill the way they were around the food, the way they looked at each other's plates and my own and Aidan's. Like vultures. On my seventeenth birthday we went to an all-you-can-eat buffet, the customers were lined up, hands round each other's waists, nuzzling each other's necks. The overindulgence was carnal as they filled their plates a mile high.

When it rained I would get an ache in my heart I couldn't explain to anyone. Aidan wasn't anyone to talk to. He barely said anything unless it was about people who pissed him off. He would wait till I was happy about something then he would launch into a tale about someone he once hated. He said he was happy for me, that I had him, because if anyone ever treated me badly he'd make sure they were sorry. He said, sure wouldn't I do the same for him.

I said I would.

I had to leave my work in the canteen, couldn't keep a drop of fluid down. I was brought into hospital and put on the drip. The nurse told me her niece had hyperemesis gravidarum too.

What's that, I asked. Morning sickness?

No, she said, this is morning sickness like a hurricane is a little bit of rain, but it means the baby is getting all it needs, only problem is you have to suffer. She pursed her lips thoughtfully. Are they looking after you at home? she asked.

I told her I had Aidan and I also had Les, who wasn't taking money off me anymore.

What about your mother?

What about her? I said.

The nurse said, We all need our mothers.

Maybe we do, I said, but I live with my husband.

Your husband? she said. My god, I thought you were a kid.

Nineteen, I said.

You really need to start eating before we can send you home.

But I can't stop barfing everything up, I told her.

I hate this child, I thought. It didn't even feel like a child, but a disease. I was dying. Months later when I went into labour, my pj bottoms were drenched in blood that didn't belong to either of us. I prayed for the baby to die. This baby is dead, I told Aidan.

That's because you were drunk last night, stupid bint, he said. It's gonna come out with a red face like an alchie.

Red face. He did alright. He got stuck, shoulders in the wishbone of my pelvis. Aidan waited in the hall. Do I smell alcohol off you? the doctor asked me.

Don't be ludicrous, I told him. He had to make an incision, give the baby an assisted birth. My mother wants a girl, I said, but I know it's a boy, all the trouble he's given me.

You might be right, the midwife said. Then they held him up. That red face wailing.

The first chance I got, two weeks later, I begged the canteen to let me back. I was scared to be left alone.

When I worked, my mother and Les would stay away from the house. The minute I was home round they'd come. I'd be elbow deep in laundry and she'd start, I didn't come round to talk to your back.

When do I get the chance to catch up on all this? I asked them as I sat down.

Aidan hated to see them. He went out to buy a paper. My mother told me I looked like shite. That my hair was like rats' tails and the house a tip-head.

Tell Aidan, I said, sure I'm out working.

Les scoffed. He's fit for work, that fella, he said.

They told me I needed to kick Aidan into touch. I asked if they wanted to hold the baby, my mother said her hands were probably dirty, Les said he had a cold coming. It was a Monday. Les was shaking like a shitting dog. Shaking with the thought of Tuesday coming. My sister came to visit too. She did lift the boy, but she started and all, telling me a man shouldn't look after a child.

Sure Dad raised us, I said.

How fucken dare you, my mother said. I earned the crust and cooked it, *I* cleaned the fork you ate it with.

They left. It was the first time I remember doing what I did. It started small. A nip on the boy's velvety thigh. When Aidan noticed the bruise come up that night, I blamed my sister. They're not welcome in my home anymore, Aidan said and we went to bed.

I missed that all those years I was away. We always had that thing between us. He looked at me like the sun was behind me. I hated to think he would look at another woman like that. I hated to think of myself with another man.

My past made me feel unfaithful. But when I married, I married for life.

Dannii was younger than me. She had a life in Wales before. Dannii told me nothing about it. She never told me if she was straight or gay, married or single, had kids or not. That's the best kind of person to be around inside. Do you know this song? she would say and hum the tune, lightly holding the ping pong ball in her hand. You could see that she lost herself in the memory of a tune. Her eyes would glaze.

You'd need to sing it to me, I'd say.

She never would. Nah, she'd say, don't matter.

I assumed she wanted to blend to the walls. Dannii covered her face with her hair. I could see she hadn't always blended and that had been the problem. Dannii was happy to do her time in a different country. Most girls like home soil under their cell, the home sky above. Dannii bounced the ball on the table, batted it toward me. She asked me how many months, weeks, days I had left. I told her and tried not to take any pleasure. I was going and she was not. I said I'd visit but I don't.

Dannii avoided me at the end, like I'd done to Ruth. I gave her a wave on the morning I was going. She pretended she didn't see. It made me think of my high school reunion just five years after I'd left there, how I'd tried to convince myself no one recognised me because I'd bleached the ginge out of my hair, then I realised it: I never applied myself at school. Who would have remembered me? I didn't remember many of them.

I had the girl by then too. When I got home from the reunion and I lifted her. She cooed. Aidan, I told him, she's got a god-almighty lump coming out on the side of her head.

He said, She hit her head on the doorframe when I was carrying her into the kitchen.

I remembered that defence.

Months later Aidan had to go to his mother's house, she needed him to pull apart the old dilapidated garden shed. The boy was playing me up, trying to bite every time I scolded him. Nothing I said was going through. He could hardly talk properly. I couldn't make him out. Maybe he was frustrated. You're not allowed to bite me or your wee sister, I told him, how would you like it if I bit you? I said and I lifted his arm and sunk my teeth.

He nearly squealed the place down. Bad mummy, bad mummy, he said. Me tell daddy, you bad.

The girl started then and I got the two of them, locked them in the room. Went out to calm down. When I came back my mother was there with Les, letting themselves in with the spare key. They asked where the kids were. I said Aidan had taken them. Thankfully they'd cried themselves to sleep and didn't make me out a liar.

That night the boy was playing with a toy, he was trying to hit me and the girl. I took the toy off him. Is this what you're trying to do? I asked him. I hit her over the head with it. Is this it? I hit her again. See what you've done, you stupid boy!

The lump came out like they do in cartoons. When Aidan came home I told him she hit her head when I was walking out of the door. I tried to deny the bite mark. I said maybe it was my mother, or Les, they'd been round. But Aidan could tell. He told me he would divorce me if I ever did anything like that again.

The social worker asked about my mother, about my father, about Aidan. She asked me if I understood that there had been complaints. They hadn't been from Aidan. They were assessing the two of us. She said, We've received a call in regards to a day last month when you had the kids to the park.

I don't know what you're on about, I told her.

She read from her paperwork, It says here that you dragged your son by the arm the whole way through the park, even when he was scraping his knees on the ground.

That's ludicrous, I said.

Also, there have been calls that you leave the kids alone in the house and take the bus into town.

The kids were upstairs napping. She asked that I bring them down. The boy and his bite mark and scabbed knees. The girl and her cartoon lump. The social worker looked at me like she was trying to see something in the dark.

We're going to have to take the children temporarily, she said.

I helped her get their things. Aidan was out. I knew he'd be distraught. I could make out like I'd put up a fight. Will this be in the papers? I asked.

That night I tried to console Aidan, draped my arm over him but he turned his back. You have ruined my life, he told me.

He refused to live in the Salvation Army lodgings we were offered.

There were other families there getting help, all under supervision. Other families going through similar things to us. Aidan refused to see we were anything like them. There were other kids for our two to play with. Those families had help with laundry and bills paid for them. I wouldn't feel dangerous there.

During the day Aidan acted like I was dead to him, and at night he took out his anger with sex that meant he really hated me but felt like he really loved me. But I liked being part of a couple. That's how I gauged the right way of things. I'd say something too far. Aidan would reel me in. Love keeps you straight.

Cathy came back to haunt Heathcliff. I read that book nine times. Even if Aidan had another woman by then, I knew he was bound to compare her to me because I was his first love and the mother of his children. He would always love me. He would always want me to love him. I did and I do.

After the kids were taken, I lost the job in the canteen. My mother was disgusted but not disgusted enough to take the kids in. Aidan could have split from me and fought it. He reasoned that men never got custody. He didn't try. Didn't believe he could. That's when I thought we'd get over it.

When I was pregnant the third time I was numb. It came back to me like heartburn how I'd thumped the tight drum of my belly when I was sick the first time. How it could maybe explain why the boy wasn't very smart. I was working in a sticker factory. When I felt nauseous from the stink of glue, I would have to sit on my hands.

My mother phoned. Are you seriously going to have this baby when you mistreated the two you already have? she said.

I owe it to Aidan, I said. The kids were being adopted, it would take years for the trial. Anyway, don't act like you care now, I said.

Les is gone, she said, I could hear her sucking off her cigarette. He's taken up with some whore. I don't want to ever hear you call him Dad again, as long as I live.

My mother wanted me to come round for a Sunday Chinese like the old days. She said Aidan could come if he wanted, could I get the order on my way over. I went alone. She barely looked at me. We sat silently. My sister came into the room, she was putting the back on her earring. Right, cheerio, she said and lifted her car keys from the hook.

My mother's face was suddenly putty and her mouth had lost its shape. Do you want a drink? she said.

Is this a test? I asked her.

Fanta. Fanta is what I'm offering you, she said.

I've stopped drinking this time round, I told her.

You mean you've stopped *starting* to drink this time round.

My mother was right only a few times and that was one of them. I was never much of a drinker when I wasn't expecting.

She picked at her spare rib. She was wretched looking. Then she went to the sink to wash her hands, sat back down and lifted my hand into hers. Why did Aidan not come? she asked me, now tell me the truth.

I pulled my hand away like I'd been burnt maybe because truth is seldom painless.

Aidan hates you a lot, I said.

She tried to touch my face.

Stop it, I told her, I don't understand what you're doing.

I just want to hug my daughter, she said.

I told her, It's you, you are why I didn't know how to love my children.

She groaned. You've always blamed me and Les for all your problems.

She always made me doubt what I knew to be true.

I don't know what it was that made me up and leave, but I was grateful for it. At home I sobbed in the shower. Afterwards Aidan said, Do you have to go to work tomorrow? I want to take you out for lunch.

We went for some pub grub at Foster's. We sat in the beer garden. People loved it because they could smoke there, they stubbed their fag butts into the window boxes with the trailing ivy and red and pink cyclamens. It shone, the big lemon sun, the whole time. Aidan held my hand protectively when people stared. I could feel him angry with everyone, not just me.

When the baby came I tried. She was colicky and griped and griped. My mother would take her out for walks in the pram. She said my sister would like to come on one of these walks. I said they could do as they pleased. The social worker checked on us. Aidan wants to know where the kids are, I said.

They're with a good family, she told me.

Aidan would make himself scarce. The baby reminded him of the boy and the first girl. They'd been nothing like each other, but this one was a mixture of the two. I hated to look at her.

My cooking teacher was called Trudy. Looked nothing like any Trudy I've ever known. She never intended on working in the prison service till she found a good job doing just that. She was glad to not work restaurant hours anymore, now her kids were in school. It suited when they were young, she said. Her partner would watch them in the evenings and weekends and she would take the days.

Trudy wasn't particularly passionate about food. She saw it as an energy source. There were some that would tell her she was miserable but Trudy told them people put too much importance on pleasure.

What do you get pleasure from then? I asked her.

Little things, she told me. I like the water, I go body-boarding when I can. The water gives you some kind of peace.

Not me, I told her.

The water could be sexy and dark. All I wanted was to be back with Aidan in our scrappy little house. He didn't need to talk. He could hate me all he wanted.

He was meant to be at home that day. I was watching TV. The girl was crying. Strong invisible hands threw rain at the windows, trapping us in. She sensed I was uncomfortable around her. When I lifted her from her cot, she could feel my hand spidery on her back, she straightened out, threw her head side to side. Why can't you just settle? Everything's easy for you, I told her.

I felt like calling Aidan home for a moment. Then the child calmed, she closed her eyes. I put her down and looked out of the window at the postie delivering letters. I ran downstairs to intercept him, but the letterbox rattled and she started to scream. I'd never seen that postie before. He smiled at me in the window, water dripping off the hood of his raincoat.

Don't you smile at me, you bastard, I whispered.

He dawdled on down the path to the next house.

I lit a cigarette and stood in the yard, umbrella in one hand. It's okay to let her cry for a while, I told myself, count to ten. Count, just breathe. Just... Rain pattered off the gutter. She was making a sound like gasping for air. Her room was pink with daisy stencilled walls. There was a nursing chair from the mission's charity shop, a bumper around her cot so she wouldn't hit her head on the bars. Her eyes were red, her face redder. She didn't want me to pick her up. She didn't want to lie down.

I need you to check for a pulse, the woman told me on the phone, and I asked her how. Can you feel her wrist, her heart? Can you put your fingers near her mouth and nose and feel if she's breathing?

I said, There is a little bit.

She said, The ambulance will be with you shortly, and I sat down, the baby across my knees, her fingers curled around my one finger.

She was an ordinary baby. She had cradle cap along her hairline and rough patches of eczema on her cheeks. Isn't she gorgeous, people would ask me. They watched my reaction when I agreed. They secretly worried about her, that I would do the thing I did.

In the ambulance they asked me what happened, I bowed my head. I said, She was fussy, I don't know, I couldn't listen to it anymore. My bottom lip collapsed into my mouth and my head doddered like an old something. I thought about Aidan sitting with her those hospital days. She refused to let me see her go.

Trudy said my qualifications would see me in good stead, if the degrees were too wishy-washy there was always my cooking course, that there were always places looking for staff and I should start thinking about life after. I told her I'd always had a plan. Trudy told me her church had become a coffee shop, they all had to become businesses to survive. She didn't tell me where she lived, which church was hers. She wished me well as I went.

I was on my own, no family network when I got a bedsit. The next day I was walking through the town when I saw small round tables in the window of the church and the door open. I went into the chemist for some tester makeup, a spritz of perfume. It wasn't one I'd ever had in the past, that Aidan would have bought for me for birthdays. I wondered about the social workers, what they'd say if they could see me going through the doors of a church.

Churches don't turn you away. They are a home for the homeless. Friends on tap. In church they asked me if the minister could come round. Yes, I said. You have to say yes.

It didn't take him long to get to the point about the tithe. You have to give the church ten percent of you if you want a piece of it. He had direct debit forms with him. What is ten percent of nothing anyway?

What church were you at before? he asked me.

None, I said. They are suspicious of you when you just arrive on the doorstep like I did.

I've spent time inside, I told him.

He did something strange with his jaw.

Do you have anyone? he said.

No.

You do now, he told me. So I signed the forms.

I wanted to tell Aidan I'd sorted myself. I work in the church coffee shop, I wanted to say. Do you want to go out for a meal sometime? I get off around four, does that suit you? Sometimes I'd get the bus to our old house and wonder if I should call to the door.

I knew he wouldn't have waited around for me. Aidan doesn't need a great love. Anyone will do. But maybe I could catch him on the hop.

I went to my mother's house. Les answered the door. I was only out a fortnight. It was only force of past habit. My mother came to the door, her hair cropped short. She gave me her black look. Her eyes looked huge. Come in then, she said.

I sat in the kitchen with her, Les was standing in the background. He patently hated me. His eyes were on my mother the whole time as she touched her neck self-consciously.

Your mother's had both breasts off, Les said.

Sit down, Les, my mother told him.

He did what she said. Tell your mother, Les said.

Tell her what? I asked him.

Whatever you came here to say, tell her. Get it done with.

My mother reached across the table, pulled my hair with both hands, smashed my face off the table. She released one hand, drove those knuckles into my head as if drilling my skull to the table. I got up and straightened myself. I have no one, I told them.

You deserve no one, my mother said.

I've had my punishment. I am your child, I told them, tears stood in my eyes.

You're a child-killer, Les told me.

I am that, I said, but I am a lot of other things too.

I saw Les in Foster's one night after. He tried to buy me a drink. He wanted to sit beside me. He wanted to talk to me then, away from my mother. One minute he was telling me I'd destroyed the family. That he'd been good to us. Always stood up for me. Next thing he had his hand under the table. Other hand dead by his side. You used to like this, he whispered. I was tore up.

She'll never believe you, he'd said late one August, my mother working an extra shift, my sister four then and staying with Les' sister for the bank holiday weekend. It was the tail-end of Hurricane Charley. Les told me we'd go to the shops once the rain stopped. It didn't stop. Fuck you are beautiful, he said, guiding me, hand over hand. You want me to do that to you now, don't you? I do, I told him bisected by shame and thrill. A whip of rain hitting the window.

Les and I went to my bedsit and we stood for a while. I lived in a dive, somewhere Les scanned around and found himself hard to ease there. He asked me if I liked the place. I said I didn't care one way or the other, it was better than a prison cell. I had a photo of Aidan. I kept it sitting there beside the TV, not trying to torture myself, just learning to live with it. Sometimes thinking is the opposite of moving on and sometimes, no matter how hard you try not to think, your troubles rumble on.

Do you want a drink? I asked Les.

What do you have? he asked.

Tea or juice.

No, he said.

You could hear next door's TV purring.

I liked Les better when he was younger. When I was younger. I hadn't had a man in a decade and a half. I ran my fingers through my hair thinking of the woman he'd left my mother for. The whore. Les sat on the sofa. He looked at me. He was afraid. He shook his head. I think I should go, he said. But he didn't.

I asked him to leave. Then I turned on the TV but couldn't see a thing.

When my mother died there was a knock on my door. It had been a year since my release. My sister was there with Les. Mother had been buried already, hadn't wanted me to know till it was too late for me to dampen her funeral. I asked Les if he knew who my real father was and he told me my mother had been a *bit of a girl*. Could be one of a couple of fellas.

He waited till my sister left before he got teary. I'm going to sell your mother's car, he said, the money's yours if you want it. Or maybe you want the car?

The money would be better, I said. You can let me know.

A week later I brought him a bottle of drink. He got emotional again to see me. He poured us both a drink and we sat at the table. He told me about my mother, how she didn't have it in her to love us kids. Your mum wanted a dog but not to have to walk it, he said.

I must have been the dog.

He acknowledged she was extra hard on me. I asked him about my sister, if he ever did *our* thing with her. He told me no, because she was his real child. I knew this to be true. Les put his hand on the table and stroked my fingers. He was no longer young. Neither was I. I could leave if I wanted to. I closed my eyes, felt his hand crab up my arm, across my shoulder, clutch my breast.

You are so beautiful, he said. He ran his thumb across my lips. I took his hand and kissed his fingers.

You always loved me, didn't you? I said.

I stood. He stood. We walked to the wall. I unbuttoned my trousers and pushed them to my knees. The thrill came back. The shame. I pushed it aside. He made me come, brought his hand to my neck and kissed me. Slobbery. Wet. I don't know if I could sleep with you, he said, but I'd like to give it a try.

Finding breath I said, What I'd like, Les, is for you to go fuck yourself.

I left, thinking about my dead mother, if she could see us when she haunted the place. I hoped so. Sometimes I felt her presence. I never sensed my second girl. She stayed well away.

When Les died my sister came to visit. She asked if I would like to go to the funeral. You were always close, she said, and Aidan will be there. I asked her if she thought he would talk to me. She told me Aidan hadn't reneged when she told him I was out. So I told her I would see her there. I would make sandwiches. I was glad to see my sister traipse out into the rain and hop into our mother's car. She always deserved it more.

The funeral was small, mostly Les' drinking buddies. I ended up face to face with Aidan. It couldn't be helped.

How have you been? I asked him.

He shrugged.

I asked if he'd like to meet up sometime. I thought he'd say no outright but he said nothing.

I asked, How about after, or how about now?

Do you really think you can say anything I'll want to hear? Aidan asked.

I intend to, I said.

I AM MAHORO

It all start many year ago, becaus of course dats were all story begin, not today wen he standin opposite me in de street but long time away beside a lake in Rwanda.

Thees is not de first time I seein him here. De first time I see him in England was some month ago, he was standin in my place of work purchasin coffee made by one of de otha *barista girls*. He was part of a crowd of five men like de first time. Thees time he was not shoutin but askin for a regula coffee wif hazelnut flavourin in it. He say he was in a hurry. A chill run trew me worse dan de Manchesta rain I have nown much longa now dan I eva no de African sun. Surely it was not him, I thought, but dat mouth I cood not forget, de way it shape itself roun hees orda wen he ask for soy milk—of all tings! One of hees eyes refuse to open all de way. It was him. Make no mistake bout dat.

My heels want to turn to face de otha way but part of me was to fraid to turn my back. I did not want to draw a tension but I simply cood not move. Disbeleef ran ova me like ice-cold water. De men were speakin Kinyarwanda among demselves. Really, I was great full he was in company for if he not been distractin he wood surely notice me, root to de spot, starin at him so. He took de lid of hees Styerfoam cup an trew it in de bin. I watch hot coffee dribble down de rubbery edge of hees cup on to hees fingers. Hees face did not flinch at de burn.

Irish Jacqui was in de back of de coffee shop thummin trew paper work so I cood creep bout in de doorway no longa. Her eyes leeve her page, she point toward de box of filters on de top shelf. *Mahoro, your break end minutes ago*, she say, so I took de box wif me back out to de shop front. I made sure to stan wif de basket of muffins obscurin my view of him, an hees of me. I decide dat, if he were to turn, I wood easy sway one way or de otha, dat he wood not see me. None of de men wood. I fell calm for der are times wen you can weel yourself invisible. I beleeve it.

I stood, heapin use coffee-mud into de bin, watchin dem leeve in de reflection in de chrome espresso machine. Jacqui came out to chek every one was pullin der wait. Jacqui say, *rememba to greet every customa wif a smile, chuck*. She say I cooden go rong if I do thees, dat she always startin girls who wooden be hospitable. But I was not a girl. I am small an thin an always been, but it is a long time indeed since I was a girl.

Jacqui always sing de word *smile* to me if she catch my face at peace. *If de wind changes you stay like dat*, she say. My motha use to say some ting simila, she say, *Maybe tomorrow you be sad an den no a reason to be*. Motha alway smile, even wen life was tough, as it was. She was always takin on de work of her neighbours on top of her own. Motha make sure I no how hard I need to work to stay one step forward. She wood say, *Done show your sufferin, people ignore pain, it only make you feel worse*. But is harda for some people to hide der hurt dan othas. Jacqui need not no bout dat.

I close up shop each night. It take me tweny minute afta my shift is dun. De othas complain dey arn doin it for no ting, even pretty Irish

Phoebe who is nice so much of de time, so many Irish in Manchesta. Jacqui remine dem she only pay in half-hours, dat dey been agreeable on de application. *People change once der foot is in de door*, she say. Jacqui no I stay to de deff.

I stay an watch de teenagers drinkin drinks wif skinny milk makin swirls in dem, dey wearin skinny jeans an der hair is all soft an floppy. Dey wylin away der time. I see der giggles, thread bracelits tie roun der rists, markin dem as some ones bes friend or sayin dey follow de same religion as de moviestars. Dey done see me, an wen people done see you, you can look at dem very closely. I wonda bout dates to de cinema, an bout bein kiss in de back row. I wonda what it like to be excite bout de thought of bein touch by a boy.

Jacqui catch me daydreamin, she tell me she need to head of early. She confide she like to give her chilren der baff, I wipin de surfaces wif a cloth wen she talk. I lock de door from inside, jus strip lightin behin de back wall glintin of silva machines. De window glass was speckle wif rain from early in de day. I picture him out in it, hees skin wet from outside, not from de sweat pourin out of him.

I look at my reflection agains all de still. I look de same as wen I first see him, my face froze it seem, an I understan why Jacqui is so insisten I keep my mouth in a smile shape. Even wen I try to, it do not change my eyes. I start tellin myself, *Mahoro lady, you must practice smilin in de mirror at home*, tho I wone show Claudine.

Afta I stan at de otha side of de counta were I seen him early dat day, tho many shoes been in dat spot since hees. Claudine wood say I jus makin tings worse if she see me. I touch de counta were I seen him lean as he give hees order, as if I wood pick up some six sense from were he place hees hands — de hands dat were last to touch my fatha, before mine.

Afta my fatha was kill I had no motha to turn to. You see my motha die in 1992 of stomake pains. Before I come to Manchesta I think dose pains were some ting in relation to all her pregnancies, of which only I survive. Now I am tank full my motha die before she cood see her neighbours turn one agains de otha. Before de wispas turn to dark, evil deeds.

I wen home an tole Claudine I seen dat man. I new Claudines face wood sqint like de sun was in her eyes an her top lip wood rise, exposin a row of shiny pink gum. She was curl up on one end of de sofa teasin her hair, de scar from de top of her jumpa run up her neck splittin her chin like a plum, de skin on it like silk in de TV light. She suggest dat my magination was takin me away wif it, perhaps. It was part of de tings we neva speak bout, like de flat side of her chest, why its outline is rugged trew her warm nit jumpa material an more obveeus in her skimmin cotton nightgown.

Talkin wif her mouth full of potato crisp Claudine begin tellin me a story bout a British solja home from war in Afghanistan, she was foldin an refoldin a crinklin plastik bag, talkin bout how he was walkin along de street an den he here some ting terrifyin in some ting humdrum — like a car backfirin — an it make heem fall to hees knees, cova hees ears, an quake like a scare child. *Even de brave soljas feel fear,* she say. But she neva mention what make her fraid.

Claudine become English. I shooden been surprise wen it been de guts of tweny year since we left home an join up here. She wear designa labels tho dey past season an some are nock of, like she forget our tradition. Claudine neva marry an neitha do I. England was what we marry — de idea of new starts. You need no men for dat. Men dun tings to Claudine dat she keep to herself. Men take my fatha from me, an laff in my face.

Claudine say she cood see de evil inside people, it diden mean it was de same evil she an I already seen, usually some ting lessa. But Claudine say it was dangerus, if we all wen roun maginin to see de ghosts of our past, den maybe tomorrow I be accusin her to. She say, *We out of coffee an how can dat be wen you work in a coffee shop, Mahoro?* She diden understan dat it waft up my nose all hours of de day, dat wen I return home I want to feel flat an cold. Claudine got up den an head for de kitchenette. She fling two teabags into a little silva pot of water an slide it on to de warmin stove. She laff before askin me in her bes Mancunian accent, *Fancy a good English brew instead, Chuck?* An I cant help but giggle den.

*

Perhaps I shood neva of mention him to Claudine. It seem to send her mine in ova time. She begin to talk bout her village more an more, like our join memory had de hand lift of it an been allow to bounce of de walls of our bedsit. Claudine ask me from time to time in de weeks afta he walk into de coffee shop, *Mahoro, have you seen de cockroach again?*

No I have not seen dat man, I spit. To him I was cockroach. He had shout *inyenzi* before tryin to crush my soul. Claudine return my look wif de one only she, I, an de otha Tutsis cood no, it say, I no what you sayin, we done need to speak of it. Afta dat Claudine dodge de topic all togetha, den a few week ago it was Refugee Week at de community centa. Claudine an me wen along an lissen to a few talks. A man der was sayin dat people herd bout de genocide, but dey did not see de fear in peoples eyes dat make life hard to keep livin.

Wyle we der we sit in silence an fell stick togetha, but wen we left for home I say no ting bout it an Claudine jus talk bout, *What we havin for our suppa?* I think bout dose hundread days in 1994. I always have to beleeve we get der slowly by slowly. *Buhoro buhoro* are de words ringin in my head, de head dat struggle to hold much of any ting before our little English home. But here are a few tings I do recall — I recall de soil of Kigali, me feelin de grass mark my knees as I crouch beside my motha, she smilin an weedin de green bean patch. I rememba how dirt unda my nails always seem to want to tell my story for me.

Now I neva have cause to immerse my hands so. For dat I was tank full until he reappear in my life. I shood of realise my tension span was bes wen it was short. I shood let it stay dat way, perhaps.

*

Every shift I wonda if every dark-skin, muscula man is him. Some time I think I here dat voice I cood neva describe if I wen lookin from now to de end of time for de words. It had a tone dat make my hands shake. Afta a wyle I try to stay away from de shop front. I offa myself de donkey work. If Jacqui wasn der I say, *I done mine makin coffees,* an seein every one is work shy, an hate de idea of doin any ting more fizical dan handin ova pounds an pennies, my coleagues happy to let me.

I go out de back, tip de crumblin brown granules in a mound in a cardboard box, den at de end of anotha day of heem not returnin, I lock de door, turn of ceilin light an stick my hands into de coffee waste until it wedge up into my fingernails. It make my hands heavy. It remine me of my fatha.

Afta I walk home I pass Claudine on de sofa, she be readin Grazia magazine an chewin on some ting sticky like a jellatin sweety. It keep her from talkin. I go straight to de baffroom an clean my nails out wif my toothbrush an a bar of soap. I make a pot of tea. I pour de boilin water ova dose stain bristles, flick dirt away dat splatta on de mirror. My face still look no diferent, jus de whites roun my eyes are showin pink. Der are little vanes of red, dey are new. I wash away de scratches on de soap, smoovin it ova wif my fingers — circlin, circlin.

*

Today Jacqui is fed up wif her staff. She arrange a team meetin an give two speech, first to one hand full of staff, den dey go back to work — to college, or to bed — an de otha half come back to here her. I no what is comin. Jacqui remine dem of de terms dey agree to in der interview. She say, *Little Mahoro here is de only one who done complain bout lockin up.* But she done care if I close de shop alone at night, it is easy for some one like me in her mine. Some one who look so sad won be faze pullin a shutta down tho I can barely reach. Jacqui done sing *smile,* der is no ting she can say bout my demeana for I neva promise her to be unbroken.

Wen de meetin is ova Claudine is waitin at de counta for me. *Is it your lunch break now? Let us go for a walk,* she say. Outside she say dat a woman in our bildin has a visit from de police thees mornin. *She bein investigate for lyin on her immigration papers,* Claudine say, linkin her arm ova mine. We walk trew de streets for a wyle, we stretchin our legs wif no were in partikula to go. Claudine speak like she not nervus, but I no she must be for she neva come to my work before.

I say, *Done worry, tomorrow dey be accusin us.* I try to be jokin but she done think it funny. She stop in de road an shake her head. Claudine say, *Afta every ting?* De rain start up now, it is peltin heavy on us. Comin down like spears. Claudine drag me into a shop wif SALE signs in de window. A pair of blue an gray trainas she had her eyes on are now de price dey shood always been. I lean agains de window an Claudine try dem on, she ask bout half sizes for dey nip cross her feet an she sqeeze each side to show were she mean. De shoeshop door is kep open wif a plastik stoppa, I can put my hand outside an feel dose water drops splashin in my palm.

Across de street he standin in shelter dat man from de banks of Lake Victoria is here. He has hees phone in hees hand, textin some one. Its among de last of tings I eva expect to see him do wen I lay awake at night for years, relearnin not to count de hours until day. De way he smilin to himself is almost soft, I cood neva magine dat look be possible on hees face. I am seein again what took me years to blur out of my eyes, hees head — now bow like before.

Dose fingers of hees I rememba to, as dey shoot der way ova keys of hees phone, I see dem hack hees machete at my fatha, again an again. Even afta he shood of stop. I see dose olda men holdin hoes an clubs, standin behin, directin him, one of dem trappin me down on de groun, hees breff all beer-smellin an hees hands pressin an jaggin de skin of my arms, leevin big tenda broosin. I see him an de otha Hutus leavin, sayin I will live a life of heartake, *A life worser dan deff.*

Afta dey left I look for a spade to give fatha a grave so de fish wood not feed on him. I use my sandel to make a hole big enuff dat I have energy for. Dey can bury us sholda to sholda if dey come back, I think den. I cova my fatha up wif my hands like dey belong to some one else, yet I neva fell more aware of any part of me.

I forget bout Claudine until I here de retail assistant offerin sports jel for de trainas. *We come back an get dem later*, I say, fraid to take my eyes of him. He is puttin hees phone into hees pocket, wondarin bout venturin out in de rain. Claudine is bout to put up a fight until she see my eyes. *Set dem aside for me please*, she say, hangin her hand ova my sleeve, joggin along to keep up wif my pace.

I neva left on lunch before, even bein face wif him, I wonda bout de coffee shop. Will Jacqui understan if I am late back, I think. I think bout motha to, if she cood see me now wood she say dat tings are put in our paff to teach anotha route to go? Wood motha say I was a little snake once, but now I am big enuff to bite back?

I walk fast. Determine. Claudine wisperin in my ear, *Were are we goin, Mahoro? Have I dun some ting rong?* He turn into de street, pullin hees hood top ova hees head. I watch hees rain-wet sholdas an de shape of hees back, like wen I knelt in de wet, my fatha in my arms, bleedin Lake Victoria red.

My auntie an uncle an granmotha were already kill in der home de day before I watch dat man take de last person I had away from me. He hadden jus taken fatha, he take me to.

Afta I bury fatha I was so tire I cood not run. People was always watchin, dey had chekpoints of Coca-Cola crates on de pave road bout de city. My fathas friend Innocent lift me of de grass an carry me away. I no he is Hutu an I very fraid. He take me to de catholic church were he say de men dare not approach. De compound was ovacrowd wen we arrive. Outside I sit alone an watch white butterflys swimmin on waves of de air. I look at dem an still I feel num.

Innocent come an sit wif me, he tell me de militiamen are comin, dat now dey are leavin victims were dey fall. I tole him soljas left my fatha too, *Dey trew him in da lake*, I say. *Evil an den more evil*, Innocent say, hees eyes fillin wif water. People are watchin us speak. People are not noin if dey can be trustin him or de otha Hutus who have come among us again. Innocent say hees wife was Tutsi, dat de men look at de ethnicitie on her card an dey kill her. He seem to give up. It is ova for him one way or anotha, he say.

Innocents younges daughta, Mahoro, die six month before wif malaria, he press her carte d'identité into my hand, Innocent sayin I am small an skinny like she. Innocent say I *must* trust him an den he tell me to go now.

Wen I look at my dentification since, I think of him. How peculia it is dat in Rwanda I was Elizabeth. In England I am Mahoro.

*

We followin de man for half-mile now, Claudine wisperin, *Dats him,* me not noin if she mean it as a question or if she jus no. As I walkin I wondarin how it will go. De rain eases an fades away my urgence so. We done pass a police offica an Claudine done urge me to call dem.

I want to shout but I say no ting becaus I no de world do not lissen.

What if he turn to face us now an he recognise me? Maybe it will make a diference, I think. What if he eva come in de shop wen I openin a package wif a sharp blade in my hand? Will dat be diferent? I wonda if der is eva an end to our story.

He jump into a dark blue car an start up de engine. I stop walkin, Claudine sqeeze my arm. Perhaps England allows us all to become diferent people, I think.

WE WAKE WHEN WE WAKE

We wake sore, wracked up on the sofa, watched by the bloodshot eye of TV standby. Morning elbows its way in and kicks up dust, reorients it on the face of the furniture. Outside the air is stale with what has passed: the imperceptible shuffle of one year into the next. Threatening rain is the whelk-coloured sky. Dead factories lie in wet cotton heaps. A while ago this town folded like paper, yet this is the place that holds us, and sometimes the prodding finger. The accusatory wag.

Sometimes it is something else altogether.

Signs of hopelessness are everywhere we can bear to look. There are no management, no operatives, no labourers or lackeys. Certainly no microwavable success. Machinists and cultivators have left since nothing is engineered or grown, apart from the children. We wake when we wake, roll out of bed, tie ourselves in knots. The kids are kept late for arriving late, but what is there to be timely for? No one stays indoors looking at four walls, at all they own and all they don't. Souped-up Sky discs listen like ears. Roughcast cladding, crocodile cracking, Boston Terriers. People not born here come and don't stay long. Nothing exists till we do. We call ourselves a community, watch out for each other. January to December, young and infirmed, all of our lives we have looked after our own. You can't ask for much more than that.

Ian left his home and headed for town, his clothes pasted to him. He hardly felt the cold though his arms were bare, his t-shirt torn at the seams and splashed with blood. If Ian had been in his right frame of mind he would have noticed the by-passers in cars, the people coming home from night shift, and in taxis business folk heading to catch their morning flights, slowing their shared towrope to watch Ian. The cars like links of a platinum and pewter chain.

The pavement felt as though it was going forward with him. On his rubbery legs Ian walked, intoxicated by the nostalgia evoked in every square inch of his small town. He passed the park where he'd had his first proper fist-fight at twelve years of age, and then behind the park, in the alleyway, he'd lost his virginity to Cherith at sixteen. Then there was Foster's, where he was headed, where he first laid eyes on Dominique.

That was a Friday night six months before. Ian had sat with his mates supping cheap ale. Once Dominique's friend had left to go to the gents, Paddy shouted to her, Tell your mate to do one. You want a real man.

Dominique gave him a bitter look. I'll not find one hanging round here that's for certain! She sounded as angry as Ian had felt for months. He imagined she had the same ball of spite fizzing in her chest that he was always trying to choke back. Those black stones in the centre of her eyes held a mirror to him.

Paddy had chuckled to himself. I did ask for that, didn't I? he said.

No, Ian told him. She's a slabber.

Ian rattled the last coins in his jeans pocket, his round next. He looked across to the table to where she sat, a look on her face like she would quite happily punch him in the mouth. Her anger was magnetic. The guy rejoined her. Ian didn't recognise either of them. He watched as the man hitched his hand to Dominque's arm, she seemed to flinch ever so slightly yet she stared into his eyes as they spoke intensely and surreptitiously, making Ian feel as though he had no right to be in his own local with his lifelong mates, observing this intimate knot. Ian despised the look of the guy in his tight muscle-strained t-shirt, even though Ian had no right to feel resentful when he had Demi-Rose and their kids back at home.

Ian, look at your face. Les laughed. You're really hacked off.

Ian felt himself get heated again, like before he'd left home when Demi-Rose had criticised him for not being helpful, rhymed the usual about him needing to get a job to support his social life, yet Ian knew there were no jobs to be had since the factory closed months earlier. Almost a year ago now. He once taught kids to swim, but now the leisure centre was boarded up and Ian wouldn't give up his weekends to travel elsewhere for a youngsters' gig.

Ian remembered that humid night, he'd noticed Dominique straight away. She was wearing a short floaty dress that clung to her in all the wrong places — or all the right places if you were a man like Ian, whose head was steeped with all things unfamiliar and unobtainable. He could tell she didn't normally dress up like that. She looked uncomfortable and it made him glad.

When Dominique left her table she caught Ian's eye, he followed her into the corridor. Dominique was leaning against the cigarette machine in the nook outside the gents. She covered her free ear while she spoke in a low voice on her phone, drowning out the music playing in the bar. There was a hush as Ian approached her.

Yes? Can I help you? She sneered at him. He curled his lip at her like he had noticed shit on his boot. Creep, she muttered under her breath as he entered the toilets.

For a moment he stood behind the door contemplating telling her she was lucky she wasn't a bloke, but he'd never hit a woman or even threatened one. Ian wasn't about to start, no matter how low he had begun to feel. He was a lot of things, but not that.

The next morning Demi-Rose had taken the kids to her mum's, then she slunk back into bed with him. She rubbed her hand under the good shirt he had fallen asleep still wearing, her hand on his ribs. Demi-Rose kissed Ian on the neck. Are we mates again? she whispered, leaning over him to peer into his face.

Ian's eyes were two slits, his face puffy with sleep. Aye, we're mates, he said rolling over to put his face into Demi-Rose's hair. He imagined it was Dominique's. Ian wrapped Demi-Rose's hair around his fist while they had sex, carrying on his dreams that had recurred all night. Afterwards, Demi-Rose asked, Is it my turn now?

Ian turned his back. When Demi-Rose sighed, Ian heard it. He tried to ignore her disappointment.

*

The toes of Ian's boots were scraped, he could see this as he faltered along the asphalt. The leather was shot. His *dancing shoes* Demi-Rose called them, she always knew if he was going out on the lash if they were on his feet. Ian's jeans yawned at the knees. Demi-Rose had taken to them with nail scissors and the cheese grater to make them look *designer*, snipping and fraying edges. She'd seen an article that inspired it in one of her magazines. Now the jeans were massive gaping gobs with bloodied broken jaws.

He traipsed across the road feeling the breeze blast down his shins. The tightness of dried blood cracked open into a cold sting as Ian tripped up the kerb. He couldn't get Dominique out of his mind. Ian could only see that girly dress. The strange marriage of it to the woman inside.

*

It was three months till Ian saw Dominique the second time. Alright, Gobshite? was how she greeted him. This time she had a puffa jacket on. She sat smoking outside the front of Foster's. Ian joined her. Without a word she lit his rolly with her orange Bic lighter. Roll ups? she asked with a laugh.

Ian wouldn't tell her it had to be. Since he was relying on benefits how could he justify cigarettes anymore?

Have a proper smoke, she told him, handing Ian one of her B&Hs. The collar of Dominique's coat sat high beside her ears, her hair tied up. Ian looked at the ponytail.

You haven't much to say for yourself tonight, have you? she asked.

I have plenty to say for myself, Ian said.

She took a draw of her cigarette and kept his gaze, unfazed and comfortable despite his glower. Tell me something then, she said. Tell me something nobody knows about you.

You're a bit of a head-case, Ian said. He thought she was a high-maintenance kind of girl, like the ones he always seemed to pursue when he was younger. Just like Cherith, Dominique had trouble written all over her, yet he was still pulled more than willingly up that gradient.

I've never had a guy call me a head-case before, said Dominique.

Been many, has there?

Mind your own, she swiped.

Oh, I see. But you want me to tell you something about me that nobody knows.

Alright then, don't. I don't give a fuck. Dominique stubbed out her cigarette, about to walk back into the bar.

Are you with your fella tonight? Ian asked before she could leave him outside alone.

What fella? she asked.

The one from the last time I saw you. Michelin Man. Protein Shake. Whatever his name is.

She cast an eye over Ian. Who wants to know?

I do.

And who are you when you're writing home?

Ian, he said.

She offered a hand and he took it in his, her palm gentle, succumbing. Ian held it a moment too long. I'm Dominique.

Fuck away off! Ian pulled his hand back to take the cigarette out of his mouth, it wavered between his teeth. You aren't called Dominique!

She frowned, then laughed, crossing her arms across her chest. Dominique jutted her jaw. There was something in her confidence that made him want to knock her down, but only because he thought she could take it. Why would I lie about my name?

Okay. Then where'd you get a name like that?

My dad's French.

Dead on! Ian laughed. Aren't the French said to be... refined?

Dominique shook her head. I'm a head-case *and* unrefined?

And I'm a creep?

Okay. She sniggered. Is the slate clean?

Alright, *Dominique*, Ian said in an awful mock French accent.

Dominique lit another cigarette, taking a long draw of it and then releasing smoke and melting into a smile. Michelin Man, as you call him, or Stuart, as I call him, was trying to get back together with my cousin. I was being go-between. She looked at Ian who stayed silent. Stuart had just got out of hospital after slitting his wrists. I wasn't in the mood to take your nonsense that day, is that good enough for you?

Ian glanced at the sky, saw the stars had emerged without him realising. Shit, he said. Did they get back together?

Would you take back an emotional blackmailer?

No.

Good, Dominique said, you take no crap either. That's what I like about you.

Ian was surprised to hear her say it. The people who liked him had always been there, they had all grown up together like a strange interchangeable family, lumped together through time served and duty. Like Paddy and Les, though Les was older. Like Demi-Rose in many ways.

Ian reached over, cupped Dominique's face and kissed her in the street, in full view of his neighbourhood with the very valid possibility people who knew him could be passing. Let's go to yours, Ian said, his forehead pressed against hers.

She tapped her finger like a metal detector on Ian's wedding band. You didn't mention that, she said, edging away. Ian watched her go inside. The oversized coat, like that of a man, made him green with envy. He finished his smoke then went back into the bar, but he couldn't see her anywhere.

The next week Demi-Rose took the kids to her mum's so she and Ian could have a night together. She said they were always in each other's pockets and indoors. She complained they never went anywhere as a couple. After the pictures, she wanted to go to Foster's for a nightcap.

Alright, just the one, Ian said. We're hardly made of money. He vexed that Dominique would be there, that she would go off like a cocked pistol, with Demi-Rose following after. Really, he had only seen Dominique twice in months. It was unlikely she would be there.

They took the table by the door. Ian watched the window. Demi-Rose spoke about how the kids needed new school shoes again after one term. It gets to me, Demi-Rose said, when you don't listen.

I'm listening, he replied.

You seem like you're in a world of your own, she said. I don't think I can take it anymore. Demi-Rose's eyes filled up. Ian flitted his gaze around the bar to see if any of the bar staff were looking. Gossip was spread around the town almost as fast as chlamydia.

Dems, stop that, he told her.

We can't go on like this, she said. You're always down here while... Where am I? Do you even notice?

I do care, Ian told Demi-Rose, holding her hand then pressing it as though it was a volume switch that pressure would quieten.

I need to say these things, she said. I've been reading about marital problems lately. We aren't communicating. You never listen to me. She freed a long dissatisfied sigh.

Ian saw Archie enter Foster's then. Archie had landed on his feet with a job for the council. Ian couldn't be dealing with his patter and Demi-Rose's meltdown too. He jumped up and strolled out of the door past the spot where he'd asked Dominique to take him home just a few days before. For an instant Ian wondered if Demi-Rose was right, maybe they were meant to be with different people. Only the thought of his kids being raised by some other clown stemmed the notion. Ian fumed up the street while Demi-Rose hurried behind him.

Ian! she bawled. I need to talk to you!

He marched on. She arrived home in a taxi ten minutes later. If you think that I'm gonna chase you like a teenager, you can think again, she said before running upstairs. The crash of the bedroom door shook the house to its base.

*

Ian's head ached as he stumbled past the courthouse. One evening, years ago, Demi-Rose and her friends had stood on those steps, smoking and sipping bottles of coke with vodka in them, as though they were the ultimate bad girls laughing in the face of the law, just months from being legal drinkers. Ian knew her to see from school but he'd been too busy pursuing Cherith to notice Demi-Rose properly.

Cherith had just had the termination and was resting up when Ian and Paddy went to Foster's to commiserate and mull over the close-call, the being made responsible at too young an age.

The irony was never lost on him, how he'd ended up tied, the night he'd just narrowly escaped. That night Demi-Rose had ended up in the toilets of Foster's with him. She had given Ian a blow job and became his next infatuation while Cherith had become solemn and sensitive compared to Demi-Rose, who seemed uninhibited and carefree. They somehow traded places.

She took Ian's mind off Cherith. Demi-Rose refused to sleep with him till seven months in, unaware that she was already more adventurous than her predecessor. Ian put on an act with her, one of discontent, although really he knew Demi-Rose was in the palm of his hand. He need do very little to please her in return.

*

Foster's was open for deliveries. Look at your face, chuck, said Jacqui the barmaid from Manchester. God, that's a bad knock you took.

He touched his face and felt its stickiness, like on his knees. His hand had dried blood etched in streams between the ridges of his fingerprints. Whiskey please, Ian groaned.

Jacqui shook her head, then, against her better judgement, poured a measure into a tumbler. Rab came out from the back room. Ian had known Rab since they were kids growing up around the corner from each other. They played together, ringing doorbells, running away, smashing flowerpots, sneaking into the unlocked garage of the house on the corner of both their streets, where they used to steal wine and drink it in the park. Rab came round to Ian's side of the bar where he sat on the stool beside him.

If you've come here to talk me round, I appreciate it but I can't allow you to treat this place like that, Ian. You're still very much barred.

Ian looked around at the crumpled glass swept onto the dustpan and the bin liner full of rubble. He couldn't remember what had happened exactly, but he couldn't forget why it had. Rab, I'll pay for it, he said.

Pay your tab first. Rab yielded the whiskey from Ian's fingers, he held the glass in his palm as he walked behind the bar. Go and clean yourself up before you leave. He winced. Your face, it's open like an onion.

Ian's reflection stared back, his forehead was swollen and gaping, he could barely open his left eye. In those toilets Ian thought about him and Demi-Rose in the cubicle, he couldn't remember which one, just her face grinning, kneeling in front, hands clenched on his thighs. He thought about the first time he saw Dominique, how she had called him a creep outside that door. Then there was Cherith who had told him at the corner table about her pregnancy, the day before his seventeenth birthday. He remembered crying in the far toilet cubicle. He would never forget that.

A face appeared every so often, a child, fifty-fifty Ian and Cherith. He never wept when he envisaged the baby. It only made him wonder. It was hard to tell if things really happened for a reason or if they'd been too young, the timing, circumstances all too complicated. Cherith was the hand around his gut, always squeezing. Ian looked at his face and imagined his kids — his smiley real-life fifty-percent Demi-Rose kids — seeing his face all busted up, and their family the same. He walked out of the toilet ready to sort out everything out, one way or another.

*

The night before the fight, Ian had a few drinks alone in the house. Demi-Rose was still gone with the kids, staying at her mum's for breathing space. She was home less and less the last couple of months. Les and Paddy arranged to meet Ian at Foster's as per. They'd sat at their table when in walked Dominique with a clique of girlfriends, one was Charmaine who'd gone to the high school with Paddy and Ian.

Ian, I believe you know my cousin Dominique, Charmaine said standing over the men's table kinking with laughter. Dominique grinned from her seat.

Why, what has she said? Ian asked, instantly regretting it. Charmaine just hooted.

Ian waited for an opportunity for her crowd to scatter before he went to speak to Dominique on her own. What rubbish are you telling people? he asked.

Go away, she replied, plainly repelled by him. I'll tell people what I want to tell people, alright?

You *are* a head-case, Ian told her.

Dominique slapped him across the face. Ian grabbed her wrist while she scowled. Les sprung to his feet. Calm down, Ian. Leave the girl alone. And you leave him alone and all! Les told Dominique.

Ian released his grip and strode back to his table, everyone watching silently.

You're the psycho! Dominique screamed at him.

Ian toppled the table, drinks doused Paddy who leapt up boiling with rage. You fucken eejit, he shouted, give your head a wobble! You're acting the maggot now.

Ian swayed while Billy the husky bouncer loomed. Rab was on his way over from behind the bar. I'm going, Ian shouted before pointing at Dominique. Bunny boiler! he said. And you, Paddy, can fuck off!

Paddy shook his head. Ian, he said, you should be less concerned about this one and more concerned about your wife.

What does that mean? Ian squinted to see straight. You know nothing about my Demi.

I know a damn sight more than you do, Paddy said. She said I could teach you a lesson.

Ian remembered how he ran at his so-called best mate, falling against the glass partition into Foster's kitchen. Ian remembered pinning Paddy down as he punched him again and again, shards of glass wedged in his knees. The smashed bottle on the floor ended up in Paddy's hand, he swung it, stabbed it into Ian's forehead.

*

Ian rapped on Paddy's door. Cherith answered, looking horrified. Oh my god! Look at you too. She hugged Ian then touched the skin beside his cut. Ian recoiled, looking into her eyes, the ones he always pictured when he thought of their baby. At the time she'd said there was no other option, now what? He was tired of thinking about it. The kid might have been Ian's, but then again, maybe it was Paddy's, and wasn't it Paddy who Cherith would go on to marry?

He's still asleep, she said. Who did this to youse? She stepped back to let Ian into the hallway but he remained on the doorstep.

We did it to each other, he said.

Cherith gasped. Why would you treat each other like this?

Never worry, said Ian. He was only getting his own back.

Paddy started *this*? Cherith's expression told Ian she found it hard to believe.

These things start long before we know we're starting anything, Ian said, he turned to leave.

Cherith grabbed his arm. What's that supposed to mean? What did you say to him?

It's fucken dominoes, he said shrugging her off. Nothing more.

THE PARENT TRAP

Sundays are the pictures. Dad's as chatty as a vent on the way to the matinee. He asks me about school. Dad tells me, These are the happiest days of your life. Ask anyone.

He asks if I have a girlfriend, always on about girlfriends my Dad! But he's just raking. I'm too young for all that business. Ah, sure you're in big school now, he says reversing his blue Polo into a space with one hand on the back of my headrest, his torso is twisted but his legs are straight. Both halves of him could come apart.

He calls himself The Weekend Dad, which sounds great because before he left home we never saw Dad at the weekends, ever. But yesterday he watched my footie team play. For months he's stood, hands in pockets, making nervous skinny smiles at people who nod at him. But yesterday he was hyper, waving his arms, shouting at me to get up front, shouting at the referee for disallowing one of our goals. When he started swearing his head off, the men were all patting him on the back saying, Fair play to you, Rab.

They started chatting after that. And we won.

*

Dad pulls the brake on. He pauses, even though the cinema is chocka. The film's a new 3D release. I know from the look on his chops he's about to start.

Don't be worrying, is how he starts, which is daft because now I feel myself get all worked up. He laughs at my face, which must look pretty amusing. No. No. I said don't be worrying.

Okay, I say, but I'm confused.

Never mind about your ma and me, son. We're adults. Can take care of ourselves.

They've been split up since New Year, the way people quit smoking, so forgive me, but it's hardly hot off the press.

The queue's getting wild long. I have my finger on the button ready to pop my seatbelt out, to try to hurry him up.

It's just, son, sometimes people need their space, Dad says, he does a little arc in the air around him with one finger. I want to tell Dad not to get hopeful. In school last year we were taught that proverbs usually contradict each other, like: strike when the iron's hot, and look before you leap. I think about proverbs a lot. If Dad's thinking that absence makes the heart grow fonder, he ought to remember that out of sight is out of mind. I wonder if I should tell him, but I think he already knows.

Your ma and me had our first date here, Dad says.

I let my arm go limp by my side. Here we go. It was *The Parent Trap* they went to see. Not the remake. That came a few years later.

It was *The Parent Trap* we went to see, he says. Not the remake. That came a few years later.

I tell him I know. There's no point reminding Dad that Austin from school was here on Tuesday night and got turned away, I just told him that before we left Granny's (which is where Dad's living again), it was the reason Granny said, Well then, you two boys had best shift yourselves pronto, as she cleared my sleeping bag from her sofa and re-scattered her cushions over it.

I know what Dad's doing, with his talk about Mum, he wants to see if I remember the game we used to play when he would come home on Sunday evenings completely steamboats, Mum always pretending he wasn't there. I won't play it again. Not now. I did when I was little, but as I got bigger I just joked along to see him make a fool. Now it's not funny anymore.

Dad would start the whole thing off by saying, The first time I saw your mum was on the bus. My line was always, Did you sit beside her, Dad?

I didn't.

Who were you with?

Sally Gooley.

Who was Sally Gooley?

The old girlfriend.

What did you do when Sally Gooley got off the bus?

I went and sat beside your ma.

Did she speak to you?

No, she ignored me... like now.

What did you say to her?

I said that she was a fine-looking woman and if she didn't let me take her out for a drink, I'd throw myself under the wheels.

Last time I took part, Mum was nursing the baby. I got to the line about her speaking, Dad said, She ignored me... like now, his eyes well tanked-up, verging on pervy-looking. He pulled at her arm. Mum started screaming, so did the baby. I don't know who started first but all three of them had furious redners on them.

You nearly made me drop the child! she roared.

Dad took himself into the kitchen, stooping like he was going to get a clip around the head. Mum followed, not caring that the baby was mid-feed and getting hysterical for the boob. She was shouting,

Have another baby, Cathy. I'll have a reason to quit the drink, Cathy, putting herself in third person then changing her name. Muggins here listened to your promises. Well, let me tell you, Muggins is done with you.

Dad limped off, he must have twisted his ankle — or maybe it was more his pride that was hurt, and it just manifested itself physically, like when Granny says stress manifests itself in her motions, that she's never been so regular since Dad went sober. Dad skulked off to his weekend bed on the playroom sofa: it's just a spare room I used to have all my toys in until I got bigger and my toys got smaller and were carted into my bedroom. Now the space belongs to the baby. He has soft toys and ride-alongs in the playroom. Mum's raging she gave all my old toys away.

Dad takes his driving glasses off, fumbles them folded into the case that's attached to the car ceiling. Snaps it shut. He's crying. Dad's looking out of his window. I think he doesn't want me to see him in tears, then he looks straight at me and I think that maybe he does.

Your ma will think it's deadly you scored the winner yesterday. Man of the match, eh? Dad sniffs. That referee got his face reddened, didn't he? See all the women giggling at what I said to him? Your ma would've giggled too. Dad sighs. Your ma loved a good laugh.

Mum laughs all the time, I say, and the reason why I say it is that just before Dad came to collect me on Friday, I was in the living room with her, the baby was walking about and fell on his bum. When he put his hand to his head I said, D'oh, like Homer Simpson. Mum nearly wet herself, so I kept saying it, and the baby kept slapping himself gently on the forehead. Mum was saying, You two are some craic. Smashers, aren't you both? Squeezing us, looking sad because Dad was pulling up outside. Weekends are her time off work in the housing scheme, she would like to do the fun things, all three of us. She bought me a mobile phone for my birthday, she said any acrobating from Dad and I was to call her to come get me. The baby stays at home. Sure your dad wouldn't know what to do with him, Mum said. He'd be sitting in his own muck and your dad wouldn't smell it.

Sure Granny's there, I said.

Mum thought about it. No, she's not a great one for teaching boys. Take a look at your father for proof.

I look at Dad. His face properly crumples. I know there's no chance of seeing the flick now. Besides, the beginnings of things are the best bit. No point now.

At the start of the school year I had no idea who was going to be a pain and who was going to end up being a mate. Our first day, we boys all sat scanning each other, and unless someone was a complete nerd-looking fella I was thinking he might be alright. Everyone was beaming nervously but the teachers had right grumps on them, especially Mr Kirkcaldy, the closet baldy. Mum told me later that they were most likely okay, just laying down the law from the outset.

You have to give people a chance, she said. Jameson College is like a blank canvas, you can make it as good or as bad as you want. You get out what you put in, then she muttered someday maybe she would too.

I ask Dad if he wants to go for a kick-about instead. He says, Aye, alright, so we leave the cinema complex and make our way over to the green. I take my football from the car-boot and we have a penalty shootout, winding our jumpers into goal posts.

I wasn't a bad wee player you know, tried out for Liverpool FC's under 18 squad, says Dad.

While he's talking I kick the ball through his legs. Nutmeg! I shout.

He waggles a finger at me, shakes his head in a *you're-in-trouble-boy* kind of way. I've never seen him grin so hard. Dad pushes me aside. He scores a goal then robot dances like he thinks he's Crouchy or someone. The absolute eejit! After an hour Dad says he's out of puff, he's delighted though, he wouldn't have had that in him a while back. At the house he bumps the Polo up the kerb. There is this one kid in year four who is a complete class artist, I'm telling Dad all about him. He's not even listening. I can tell because of the amount of uh-huhs he is saying.

I'll come in and see youngster so, he says.

I fish my key out of my holdall. Dad walks into the house after me, in the kitchen he squats down beside the baby who's playing on the floor, rattling a potful of dried pasta with a wooden spoon. Mum's wearing her pussy-bow blouse and short skirt. She looks mortified by the big golden chicken resting on top of the oven. We used to have Sunday lunch early, now she waits for me to get back. There are two placemats set on the table, the baby's highchair has his spoon and cup all ready.

You still going to church, Cathy? Dad asks.

You still drinking more pints than you can pull in Foster's? she says. She's trying to be chilly with him, so I tell her that Dad and I just had a game of footie. We didn't just sit filling our faces with sweets. She looks pleased. So, you'll eat your lunch this week, will you? she asks me.

At the sink I wash my hands, watching my parents' reflections in the window. They stand parallel to each other, both staring down at the baby. Lift him if you want, Mum says, like he's only hers, then she adds, We've something to tell you.

I look round, think she's speaking to me because I'm usually the only other big person in the house. She has a different voice for the baby. Dad's practically catching flies with his mouth hinged open. I know by the look on his face he's hoping to hear that she's letting him come home. Everything is written on everybody's faces. Mum looks at the baby again, she coughs, puts her arms out to take him back from Dad. The news is... this young man put two words together.

Dad says, That's deadly, his tone hits the tiles.

No, he didn't say *that's deadly*. Mum laughs away her discomfort. He said *good boy*... to himself... after he'd only gone and completed an inset board... it's like a jigsaw puzzle, only simpler. The Golden Girls who look after the wee ones in the church crèche told me so, she explains to me, and I'm glad I don't have to go there these days. I feel sorry for the baby, but he likes it okay. He knows no different. Smiles at anybody who smiles at him.

Dad does his skinny-lipped smile. He mumbles, that's great, he'll be going then, but he's walking really slowly as if maybe someone will call him back, that Mum will remember that he could have left the bus with Sally Gooley but he chose her.

Mum shouts at me to remember to lock the front door. Dad lurches over to his car. He has a grass stain on the back of his shirt he doesn't know about. He sits in the car, ducking his head to give me a smile and a wave. He's trying to be happy because he won't know if he doesn't try.

Dad's eyes dart over our house like all he wants is to come back home. And I think he will sometime, that all he has to do is wait some more.

THE THING ABOUT SPIDERS

You know when there's a spider dangling in front of you and you try to flick it away but the thread just gets longer till the spider's just hanging there? No? Have you never seen that? Well, it's awful bizarre the way it happens. Sure you probably wouldn't flick a spider away like that. You look like a nice woman. Must be thinking I'm a bad bitch, but I didn't hurt the wee creature.

There it is, the spider. See? Ah, you missed it, it's away now. Went under that seat. It's alright.

You think it would've run away earlier but it waited, then the spider let itself down, dead gentle to the ground, like a lift going through the floors of a shopping centre. And off it scampered away, just a second before you sat down there beside me.

It makes you wonder, doesn't it now, how clean the bus must be. They don't clean buses enough, I reckon. I mean, it looks okay. There's someone's ticket on that seat, and up at the front in the wheelchair area there's an empty crisp packet. They're tidy but not really *clean*. When have you ever seen a person clean a bus? I never have. Maybe they *do* do it at night. I never really thought about that.

Not everyone says spiders are a bad thing, sure they eat the flies and the flies eat dog shite — I mean muck — so it's okay to have some around. I remember someone saying that.

When my sister Emma was visiting me once, years ago, she saw a spider in my room. Sure she hardly ever does visit any more. She said, I want these cobwebs gone the next time I'm here and I want the weeds pulled out of that front garden. Do you hear me? Tell those ones working here I say it needs done.

I told Rennie the caretaker what my sister Emma said, we were down on our hands and knees taking out the weeds. Rennie's the one who told me the thing about spiders, that they wrap everything up nice. That's why I didn't kill the spider. That's why I never would do that. I never mentioned it to Nancy the cleaner. She'd have told me to dust the room myself.

Flip! It's warm today, isn't it? You must be warm with that scarf on. I'm absolutely sweltered. Oh, it's not a warm scarf, more of a fashion thing, ties your colours together. I get you now! It's a hot day to be out. Out running about. Isn't it? A hot day to be out running.

That's another thing with this heat — bees are another thing that make the summer hard work. Have you ever seen this meme about bees? Client Ruth was in work, getting her dye put in, and she handed Gina her phone and said, Read that meme somebody put on the internet, Gina.

You know what it said, about bees? No? It said, if you find a tired bee, give them a spoonful of sugary water to wake them up. I wouldn't do it. I'd be scared of getting stung. Gina was holding a towel she'd just used on Ruth's hair, to drink up the water from her wash, and she stepped forward — Gina — and said, Tired bees? I'll give them a drink from this! And she walloped the wet towel off her work station.

We were all having a good laugh about the thought of her killing the bees, but Gina's has a UV zapper for that. It's on the ceiling. Hisses and pops all summer through. I had my hands buried in her client Maralin's suddy hair. She was giving out to me for letting the water dribble down the collar of her dress. Maralin was moving about too. I don't think it was just me that did it.

Client Ruth was wiping her eyes at Gina's little dance and Gina was turning to me saying, Make sure Maralin is comfortable please, Rebecca. She was telling the junior stylist Charmaine to turn the volume up on the CD player. It must have been in the afternoon.

In the afternoons we listen to CDs. Gina has a sticker on the door that says we're listening to music legally. Did you know there are laws about how long you can listen to the radio in a place of work? Thank God I only work on Wednesdays, Thursdays and Fridays because I couldn't listen to her songs any more than that. The radio's no better. You get sick of the news. Over and over. Somebody's been assaulted, somebody's been arrested. Nothing about if they were listening to the radio too long.

Gina always looks lovely. She's short like me. Always has the gel nails on. Highlights done. She wears a wrap top, black leggings, pumps on her feet. We all wear the same kind of thing: Gina, Charmaine the junior stylist and me. All black. If you get any dye on you, it doesn't show. Not that I touch the dye.

Here you go, there are my old black trousers and a couple of tops that will do you, Gina told me. Save you going out buying any.

Least she could do for you, Nancy said one day in the church kitchen. Nancy's not our cleaner anymore since she retired. I volunteer with her on Tuesdays, that's why I'm in town today, volunteering. Brenda comes too. I told Nancy and volunteer Brenda that Gina could use me five days a week and they said, I bet she could, for two pound a week, I bet she blinkin' could.

Gina doesn't pay me much, like a token is all it is, so it doesn't mess up my benefits. Twenty four hours. That's actually minus pounds an hour. Is there a calculator on your phone? Work it out. Two pound... now three days. See! That's the way it goes. People are always surprised when I tell them. You're surprised, I can tell by the look on your face. Would you have known about that? Has anybody ever told you?

Look at this one trying to get on, even though there's not even standing room. Look, the driver's letting him on. Have you ever seen anyone get kicked off this bus? Yeah, so have I.

Now, then.

Brenda used to be a nurse, she's a golden girl now. Retired like Nancy. Do you remember that programme, *The Golden Girls*? Brenda's like the big man-looking one with the gruff voice. Now, I'm not saying Brenda has a voice like that, she talks like a child, she talks like, *that's a blood-ee disgrace, that's a blood-ee disgrace.* I thought *bloody* was a swear till I met Brenda, but it can't be because Brenda's good at doing only good-living people things. *That's a blood-ee disgrace*, that's how she goes in her wee-girl *na na na na na* voice, Wanting you to work for *minus pounds*!

Volunteering is for no money at all. God pays you with His love. Some people are going to hell and I know I'm not one of them. It's not something I thought about before and now I won't have to worry about it in the future.

Nancy says I'm lucky to be able to swan about on benefits and all that there. She says, You're one lucky wee girl, no stress, no mortgage, no car to worry about putting the juice in, no phoning round for insurance quotes, no man to have the dinner on the table for, don't even have to worry about cutting someone's hair wrong, just shampoo, get the brush out around the floor and have the craic with Gina's clients.

One lucky wee girl! That's what they call me, even though I'm fifty next birthday.

God, look at you! Youthful wee face. Skin that's never had a day of stress! says Nancy. And Brenda goes, That's what we'd all look like if we had no children to worry over.

They love children and I love children too.

What I like is when they can talk to you, when they have a laugh with you, when they tell you things their parents do, like when they say, *My mummy snores like a big hog*, and *My Daddy dances when he's drunk the beers*. I love that part. Brenda and Nancy aren't too fussed, not once the children have got up a bit. It's the wee ones they love. Anybody in church comes in with a new-born, they're all over it. Love babies most. Fresher the better.

How could anybody be bad to them, they say taking a tissue out of their handbag, spitting on it and rubbing the bubbles off the babies' mouths.

God's creation. Suffer the little children.

Ah, the *wee dotes*, that's what Brenda says.

I look at the babies and they're cute — well some aren't really but don't say so or it all ends in tears — and they're of no more use than dolls. I never liked dolls much. My sister Emma would never've let me near hers because I was for taking their heads off, using them like baskets to hide necklaces in, stuffing dough in the necks. Never really interested in the wee babies either. No, can't say I ever was.

Hey! Do *you* know how to make fifteens? Dead easy, anybody can make them. Sure even Angela can. She did them when it was my fortieth. Her and her mum. Everybody from the housing scheme came to the party, the ones up in the residential, their keyworkers, our cook, the cleaning staff too. Nancy was our cleaner then. She came over with some buns. That's how I know those church women can bake.

Nancy was telling me, What it is, is fifteen digestives, fifteen marshmallows, tin of condensed milk and a bag of coconut, fifteen glacé cherries. Fifteen of this, fifteen of the other.

I already knew that sure. She thought she was teaching me something new. To be honest with you, I've been baking all my life. It's like explaining a parable to God.

Angela lives in the same house as me, she thinks I'm a saint for volunteering.

You're a saint! You're a saint! That's all you get out of her.

I was trying to get Angela to come along too, seeing she thought it was so good, but she isn't as able as me. They took it to a team meeting.

Staff said it wasn't in the interest of her spiritual development, not the same way staff accompany Amina to the mosque even though it's not their belief. Anyway, Angela's parents said no way. That she didn't understand the whole shebang.

Sorry, I'm sitting on your scarf. It is a lovely scarf. Lovely blue scarf. I used to have a coat that colour. My sister Emma bought it in the sales. Thought she'd shrink into it but she never did. She's even fatter now than she was. I went on at her for ages to give me the coat, in the end she did. I could tell she was dead jealous of me in it. My sister Emma always said she wasn't jealous one bit and if she wanted to be slim, she would do it easy. But there's no way she could've been happy like that. She wasn't even that bad then. It's the way she puts on weight, I mean, if it went on her ditties — I mean, you know, her bust — it would be better, or on her bum, but she's just got fat arms and big chunky chip legs. All her fingers — fat fat fat fat fat fat fat fat, and her thumbs: fat fat. She has our dad's build.

Now, then.

She's no dozer, my sister Emma, take when Mum went to prison. No! I mean heaven. Sometimes I go to say heaven and I say prison instead. That's mad, isn't it? You're laughing now. Everyone in the hairdressers says to me, You're a laugh, love. They like me there. It is good craic, you know... What was I talking about? My sister Emma? Oh. My mummy dying... Yeah.

Afterwards my sister Emma ended up in hospital while they reviewed her meds, but I was fine. You just get on with things, don't you?

She's dead smart, my sister Emma, has good exams and everything. She's a dietician. A fat dietician. Not joking! Tells you what's good for you and what's not. Tells me I need to stop this baking at home and going out for buns with the Golden Girls, and start eating berries for the antioxi — whatever they're called. I told my sister Emma, I thought you had to look the part for certain jobs, an ugly beautician would never survive. And hairdressers should have beautiful hair or they're in the wrong job.

Some mornings Gina gets me to sit over the basin and she washes my hair, cos she says I might have done it good the night before but now it's sitting up and I look like a rooster. And I shout, Cock-a-doodle-do! And she smacks me on the shoulder and says, You nutter, you!

My sister Emma thinks too much about food, you see. My dad thought too much too. He was a psychiatric doctor. People used to say, That's your dad's problem, thinking about things he can't do anything about. They said he worried about me. My sister Emma said he only worried about me because of the weirdy boyfriends I had and because it hung over him where I'd go after he, you know, died.

My sister Emma could have boyfriends all she wanted. Sure there was even that one who showed up at her work crying and made her lose her job. But all she did was go on about my boyfriend Hardy, that I better not be letting Hardy have sex with me or anything. That's why they sent me to the scheme, away from boyfriends. In case I got pregnant.

Me and my boyfriend, Hardy, weren't even having sex. We'd been going out for five years or seven years, something like that, and we talked about doing it. I'd been brought to the doctor's for the pill, and we had a bag of condoms too. We were even shown how to use them on bananas. What's that? Oh…Whisper? Okay. We tried once. Afterwards I kept saying to him, Did you come, Hardy? And he said, I don't know, I don't know, leave me alone. He got his keyworker to talk to me, to say he wasn't ready. Then my boyfriend, Hardy, moved back down South.

Now, then.

Once I was settled in the scheme my dad took a job away. That was years ago now, twenty or ten. Something like that. My dad died and no one knew for weeks. The neighbours realised by smelling through the letterbox. What does that mean, do you think? What did they smell? You don't know either, do you? My sister Emma got really upset about it. I said to her, Emma, you are thinking about it too much, you have to be more easy-going. Look at me, living in the scheme, working in the hairdressers three days a week, getting minus pounds an hour so I don't get my benefits messed up. I said, Do you see me moping, Emma? No, you don't. So move on.

They call the scheme *a family* but you can't just put people straight like if they were family for real. When Angela gets anxious and bangs her head on the wall and I go and shout at her, It's just the hoover, Angela. Move on! She doesn't listen. And when I pull her hands away from her ears, the next thing the staff are in, saying I should always get one of them and shouldn't try dealing with her myself. They said there were bruises on Angela's arms, and now her parents would have to be told.

Now, then.

They were fine. When her parents came that Sunday to take Angela out for her drive, they asked me if I wanted to come too. We sat on the seafront and had ice-cream from Paldi's. I got Turkish delight flavour and Angela had raspberry ripple. Angela always gets raspberry ripple. Her parents told me they trusted me to look out for her. That it took a bit of moving around but everyone was settled now. They made me promise to fetch the staff in future. I licked my ice-cream and I said I would surely.

Angela's mum told me that if I see anyone upset going in or out of the clinic, or if anyone says anything bold, that I mustn't grab them by their wrists, sure I won't. No, I won't, I told her and we drove back home.

Have you ever had lunch in Sweet Sensations? We get our lunch there on a Tuesday. That's pensioners' day. We go in for the free muffin. I don't get it free cos I'm not old enough, but Brenda and Nancy do. Sure even in a few years time they'll not believe I'm old enough. I'll have to bring a letter or something to show them my age, so they know I'm not trying to slip out of a net.

Earlier, after Brenda and me got ours, we sat down and waited for Nancy. She was late. She came in saying her husband was telling her to stay at home, interfering with her day. She told him what she did with her day was her business. Today calls for muffins, Nancy said rubbing her belly. Tomorrow calls for lettuce. When she went up to order there was only one left. Well, Nancy said to that girl Carla who works behind the counter, this is a blinkin' joke, you have written on that sign that you sell four different types and there's only *that* left.

Sorry, said Carla. We sold the rest.

Nancy went, Then I don't want it!

I mean, she took it, but she just picked at it to begin, even when I offered to swap with her. She kept saying, You're alright, Rebecca. But then I felt bad and left a chunk of mine. So after she ate hers Nancy said, Can I have a wee bit, just to get the bad taste out of my mouth? Then she said, Look, I'm actually a bit annoyed. Did neither of youse two think to tell that cheeky wee mare to keep me a chocolate muffin over?

Nancy was staring at Brenda's plate. She could tell she'd had the last chocolate 'cos there were brown crumbs all over her plate and in the ridges of the paper muffin case.

There was this woman at the next table with her wee boy. He was about seven or ten years old. She started shouting at him, If you had the life I've had, you'd know about *fair*. You don't fucken — excuse my French — you don't blinkin' know you're blinkin' living.

She was leaning over, nipping his arm. The wee boy was near crying. He was staring at the ground. I don't know what he did. I didn't see nothing. I felt like wrapping my arms around him and squeezing him tight, being shouted at like that.

Brenda leant forward and whispered so the woman couldn't hear, Listen to that. That's a *blood-ee disgrace*.

Is this your stop? No, me either, that's good. I thought you were getting up there. I'm talking your ear off. I always feel like this on Tuesdays. All jittery. Angela cracks up with me every Tuesday. I talk too much. She starts hitting herself around the head and keyworker Cathy takes me for a walk, asks me a heap of questions about my day. Then we get my work clothes ironed for tomorrow. Get my hair washed.

I'll probably not tell Cathy what Brenda said earlier in case she thinks she's nutty. Maybe I'll tell you. Brenda said, Next day we shouldn't speak, but we should lie down like we're dead. You know, make a statement.

Nancy said she wasn't getting her clothes stinking for anything, that people would think we're lunatics. My sister Emma says Brenda and Nancy are lunatics and I'm getting as bad. Three Jesus freaks together. But it's not just us who volunteer. There are men too. They just go straight there, don't come to Sweet Sensations for tea and muffins or anything. I reckon we should invite them but Nancy says her husband wouldn't like the thought of it. The men don't even talk to us. There's just two of them. They're awful peculiar. I don't think they'd come to Sweet Sensations even if we asked. But it's nice to ask and not assume, my Dad used to say that. He was a very smart man.

It'd be nice to have men about again. The scheme is women, women working on the staff. Caretaker Rennie retired one Christmas. Can't remember what year that was. There are loads of men in the residential scheme but they're all disabled. God love them! The salon is all women too. There used to be one man, Louis, and he was really gorgeous, but he was the other persuasion. You get me? I thought I liked him at the time but now I understand better since Brenda explained.

One of the men volunteers quotes the bible at the girls going into the clinic. The other one just stares at them. It gives me the willies the way he does it. I mean, I don't think he should. He's not even a Christian. He's just angry. And it's different coming from a woman. I reckon if they can't come to Sweet Sensations and talk to us then they shouldn't be allowed to stare at us. Look, I wouldn't say this to just anybody, but it's okay, woman to woman. We should be able to tell women what we think of them. They have more respect for us.

It's a good trek for me every week, isn't it? But I don't mind. The people that go there leave in a different direction from how they arrive. They must get told to do that. They get shepherded in and have friends that meet them. Brenda has followed some. One, she said, had a beautiful home, three kids. Could've had another baby fine rightly. Another one was still at school. Brenda felt like going and telling her mum the badness she'd been getting up to. *Spoilt wee bitch*, she said. She was on her R plates. Drove a lovely car.

So now I reckon, if we can follow them, they might follow us. They might, you know. So sometimes I get the train, other times I get the bus.

Hey, what do you think of all these ones on the street, the ones from Romania who play the accordion? Do you think they have cars too? Nancy says they sit there, stinking, then they get up and get into their flash cars and drive home to nice big houses. Nicer houses than she lives in. There was this woman playing the accordion when we were leaving the clinic, Nancy kicked her case out of the way. Coins spilling everywhere. She said, Blinkin' foreigners! She says blinkin' when she's angry, instead of swears. She wouldn't even say *bloody* like Brenda. Nancy's very good!

Most of the time at the clinic Nancy prays loud so the girls can hear her when they're going in and out. But I know they won't care about that. I didn't care till I started going to church. Not enough women go to the clinic. That's the truth. At times it's a real snore-fest. I mean, Februarys are good and busy, after the holidays. Lots of unwanted gifts, Brenda says.

Sometimes we get real bold ones who look us up and down and shout, Mind your own fucken business, you sanctimonious bitches! I'm sorry for all the swears, but that's what they call us. They're not my words.

This woman came today, crying. I felt sorry for her. She could have been raped, I whispered to Nancy. It's still murder, she said. Nancy says that going through with the birth is like therapy. That there's adoption sure.

Nancy wasn't always Christian, she had an abortion before. She regrets it every day she says. She wants to tell everyone they're doing the wrong thing. Listen, she knows!

The thing I like least is holding those signs: the *pictures of dead babies* signs. They remind me of how I used to walk past and get upset about them, that one time I was looking back to see what the women holding them were like. I could see one of them watching me back, shooting daggers with her eyes, like I'd done that to the babies myself. I felt guilty even though I never did. I thought she must be hateful but she wasn't, because she was Brenda you see, and I just didn't know her then to know what a good Christian person she is.

Oh look, that girl there hasn't enough money for the fare. Wonder if she'll get kicked off like that girl on the late bus. Now you'll be wondering who I'm on about. It was the night of the volunteer Christmas dinner, there was this girl, you see, she tried to get on the bus. She was blocked. Hadn't enough money. She was crying because nobody would loan her it. When I told Nancy and Brenda that Sunday in church, they said the bus driver needs to see the money, and not everyone can swan about on benefits. I said someone should've been good enough to spare her the twenty pence she needed. I mean, I would've, only I'd used all what keyworker Cathy lifted from my bank account for me. It was already written up in the Personal and Social monies book.

Next day in the salon it came on the radio that the police were looking for a man who'd assaulted a young woman. She'd been walking home alone after a Christmas party. It was on the news, every hour on the hour. I was glad when the afternoon came and Gina put her Christmas CD on.

Nancy said if it was the girl from the late bus, sure she was drunk. What did she expect would... Oh! Is this you? Is this your stop? I was going to ask you if you'd like to volunteer. They need more people for Thursdays, if you're free. Hello? What do you think? Should I tell the Golden Girls to expect you? What's your name, so I can tell them? I'm Rebecca.

SECOND SELVES

Hardy was what they called the man who lived at the top of the road in the place they called *the community*. She noticed how people held their heads at some cock-eyed angle and lifted their brows just enough when they spoke about the place, allowing the meaning of these two safe words to adjust themselves in one's imagination.

She didn't know if Hardy was the man's first name, or his last, but seeing as how she had never seen anyone acknowledge him, she wondered how they could possibly know the answer either, for it wasn't a particularly close-knit area, that is to say that neighbours certainly never invited each other in for cups of tea. She lived with her father and felt the spareness of being an only child of an only parent who was never included in the girl-talk that went on outside the school gate. Yes, she knew how her father must have felt.

Every weekday morning Hardy would be at the top of the bus queue well before her. He would be wrapped in the same padded red and black lumberjack shirt, come hail, come shine. He wore a flint-coloured beanie hat and a monotonous expression. Hardy would show his pass to the driver, who never gave so much as a fleeting glance anymore, so well accustomed to his own routine and that of this passenger, he no longer seemed to require his manners. Hardy would have sat at the very back of the bus, on the left-hand side, watching out of the window. She could see his reflection from where she sat at the front, right behind the driver, where old folk with sticks, girls with prams, always cornered her in. But luckily, most passengers got off in the city centre too, including Hardy.

One day, as she stood to disembark, she saw him, his head against the window, hat fallen over his eyes. Hardy sound asleep. She stood beside the door wishing for once she was above embarrassing herself, but sensing the small shakings of the driver's impatience, she thought it best to simply step down on to the pavement, and from there she watched as the bus took off. The driver saw Hardy too, she knew he did, in his rear-view mirror, and Hardy was taken somewhere he could not have been expecting to end up, and possibly felt very afraid when he awoke.

The dance theatre was a half-mile walk from her stop. She walked, each day, past steaming coffees and buzzing cafes with all their cooking scents. Every lunchtime without fail—apart from that one day—she would see Hardy sitting in Grafton Street, checking his watch as if he had somewhere to be and maybe he had. She had no idea.

The community was a row of uniform townhouses somehow shorter than generic two-story homes, and charging through them was a strong traffic of staff. Women in white tunics came with meals and medication. Many of the people living there had problems getting around. They were wheeled about by yet more workers, plain-clothed ones, who could have easily been mistaken for family, but weren't.

She watched shop workers tell the support staff: I couldn't do your job. It takes a special kind of person, you know.

It didn't matter that the very people who weren't designed to hear those words were right there and possibly could. The cashiers' mouths moved all around the words they imparted as though savouring the flavour in them. Hardy did his own shopping. He came and went from the community as he pleased, and didn't appear to have carers or family visits. He didn't fit cleanly anywhere.

Years before they shared their city ride, she did use to see a man shadow him, stalking behind, seven or eight feet away. Once, she and her father were returning home — him from work and her from school — when their neighbour with the inflexible bobbed hair lingered about her car, the boot left open, pretending to rummage, then approached her father to let him know that Hardy had been outside their homes shouting at the shadow man.

Hardy lost it. I had to phone the guards, the neighbour said, glancing sideways and adding, How's your daughter getting on in the grammar school?

Why don't you ask her yourself? her father had said.

The woman turned her mouth into a smile-shape and said, Just be careful of that man up there. He's different from the others. God bless some of those poor people.

After that, Hardy wasn't followed from place to place but window to window.

*

She woke up, her feet slid to the cool part of her bed sheet. Her father was sitting on the edge, his hand on her arm. Time to wake up sweetheart, he said. I have a meeting in the city this morning, want a lift? She shook her head. She waited for him to leave, then got up. Seven forty-five pulsed in green numbers on her alarm clock, her father had let her sleep late. She washed, threw a tracksuit on and gathered into her holdall some leggings and a leotard, a soap bag for her shower.

In the kitchen a note perched in the bowl in place of fruit — Have a nice day, Miss Independent. Love you, Dad.

She sipped a few mouthfuls of orange juice, then set off for the bus stop. Hardy was there, sure enough, looking at the corner of their street where the bus would emerge. He was pacing like usual. Fine red veins mapped his cheeks when she looked properly. Hardy was technically a middle-aged man, though she never thought of him as such. There was something boy-like in the energy that came off him, some scatting energy that made everyone else pretend to be busy.

She was last in the line. Three people between them. The others weren't together yet they ad-libbed into small talk, she had no interest in the topic but knew it was virtually teeny-tiny. She was exempt from discussions about the weather and soap opera plot lines, and she liked herself for it.

The sun was low in the sky. At the garden wall beside the stop, heads of red and white striped petunias bobbed like mini unpegged circus tents. She rubbed the silky petals between the pads of her fingers, until the man beside her lifted his briefcase and moved forward. She turned and saw the bus was coming, plucked a petunia from its stem to put it in her pocket. They got on in single file, flash of euros, passes and the bus began its bulky bustle, Hardy in his seat, she in hers.

Lint danced in the beam of light that shone through the glass. She stuck a finger out to shift the balance. Catching her bizarre and blameful reflection in the glass, she rested her hand on her knee. The bus stopped. People got on. Beside them, under them, the city strung out.

Hardy sat, hatted-head against paned-glass. At the point he usually did, he stood. Most of them did. Hardy walked to the front in jerking motions in tune with the stall and deflate of the vehicle. She slid out of her seat before the crowd became gluey, she stepped into the aisle, Hardy behind her. She could smell his moss-scented shirt. His metals too, that stale sweat and cold night mix.

On the street, she waited at the lights for the red man to pass the baton over to his green alter ego. Hardy waved at her for the first time, she nodded back at him in surprise, stepping forward. Hardy lunged for her, grabbed her vice-like around her arm. She looked at him horrified and tried to pull herself free when his other hand shot up. A palm flat against the air, his solemn eyes on hers, the mint-tickle of his mouthwash mingling with her fitful breath. Stop! he ordered.

Hardy pointed at a car with the hand that wasn't still around her arm. The driver looking back angrily over his shoulder at her as he sped off. Passers-by hesitated to watch them. The day froze.

Releasing his hold, Hardy told her the man had jumped the lights, his signing fingers resounding the words. He beeped his horn, he signed.

Oh, she said in a voice she preferred not to use if she could get around it, it was small and garbled and made her stand out when she didn't want to.

You could've been hurt.

She could've hugged Hardy, she thought, and she did until he tensed up and spilt her from him, and the onlookers dispersed into the street.

It's okay. Hardy shrugged, he tugged his beanie over his ears.

You sign? her hands asked, surprised how his moved like wings.

Had to learn in special school.

She'd been the only deaf girl in her mainstream. Her friends knew very little and never took her father up on his offer to find them lessons. She'd become friends with her fifty-something hearing assistant instead. How quiet, how still, life had been before dance theatre.

She nodded in her timorous way and beckoned at Hardy. Cup of tea, she asked. Chat?

Work, Hardy signed back, his low-key enthusiasm all but evaporated.

She grasped it, this chance, before they would become strangers again. When? she asked.

Hardy comes to hardy, you can come to my house, he said. I make nice tea.

She watched his lips and smiled. Hardy! she thought, his nickname clicking with her. I will, she promised him, stepping back on to the kerb and watching Hardy leave for wherever he went.

In class she placed her bag on the floor, took her place by the speaker and braced herself on it, her skin covering itself in tiny electrical beats. Through its fabric this room's heartbeat soothed her own. She remembered the red and white flower. She unearthed it from her pocket, unfolded it, held the petunia beside the speaker's precise round pores, set it on the top and watched the beautiful quiver. It was something she'd managed to capture in her own young hands. She thought all of this.

The other girls warmed up by jogging on the spot, and the sprung floor absolved every bounce, and every crazy idea.

MATRIMONIAL AGENCIES

Tomorrow Hanna will ask how my visit to Suzann and Keith's went.

A disaster, I'll say. Let's talk about something else.

Hanna will pour me a gin and a slim, put it straight in my hand, she'll sit beside me on her brown cord sofa, red painted toes tucked under her bum. I'll mirror Hanna, glad to have my mother's shoes off. She'll begin, as Hanna always does, to tell me a story which at first seems as though it is about one thing—this one *thing* being Suzann, our mutual childhood friend—but really it will be about something else.

The story, in actual fact, will be about Keith, Suzann's husband.

Shattered, I'll sit and I'll listen.

Poor Suzann is how Hanna will end the story. She will lift her glass from the table beside her and clink it against mine. To old friends.

Old friends, I'll repeat, wanting, in a way, to press Hanna for more.

How did he seem? Hanna will say.

Fucked, I'll push out through a yawn because sleeping at Suzann and Keith's means not sleeping.

Yeah, of course. He must do. And Hanna will nod. Poor Keith.

We'll both go quiet. I'll start thinking about us all. Hanna will stare at the rerun on the TV. I won't know what she's thinking but I'm sure I can guess.

At fifteen Suzann and Keith got together, Hanna started dating around that time too. Hanna always fell hard, and Suzann and I would lose her. For Hanna, over the last twenty odd years there have been a handful of people. Some men, some women. Jason was the main one she couldn't shake off, managed to drag it out for seven dead-end years, even after his engagement. Probably after his wedding. But if we're talking about strings, and I believe we never really talk about anything else — strings and the shape they give to a life — then I have mine too: two children and a life nestled inside a suburban London pocket. Sure enough there are times I've almost lost my old friends. But there are times too, when we stretch out, end up in the same place at the same time. Recently this has happened with Hanna. Even before the news about Suzann.

Anyway, back when we were younger we treated Keith like this non-male, far removed from the boys Hanna and I liked. Though, admittedly, now Keith is not a million miles away from the men we ended up seeing: the Jasons, the Simons. Hanna, Suzann and I called ourselves sisters. So by rights Keith was our brother. We spoke *boy* in his presence. Keith and Suzann would listen amused, never themselves dishing any of their own dirt. We knew they fucked the same way we knew our parents did. Hanna and I didn't want to hear about it.

Keith would rib Hanna when she obsessed over Jason, and me, he would reproach me for going out with boys because *they* liked *me*. You know, to kill time. I left for university and the girls attended universities here, at home. Keith walked straight into an engineering trade. They lived without my upheaval (or my excitement, or whatever it is I tell myself my life has been made up of, that it carries a value which is *greater than* or *less than* other people's). We like our choices to be valued, perhaps, higher than our friends', like one day we might find that there is a rent to pay on our friendships and first we'll have to know the cost, and if they're worth it.

Our foursome worked because of the alliances. I had Hanna's back. Keith had Suzann's.

When she died — when Suzann died — there had been a thing with Hanna's phone. Was broken or was lost. Anyway, all her contacts were wiped. I'd happened to text Hanna from a training course I was on in the States. She told me she'd been trying to call my home and couldn't remember my company's name.

At Hanna's I'll sip my drink as we go over the conversation we had when I was back in that air-conditioned Vegas room, everything reeking of smoke, when I got back into bed and returned Hanna's mound of missed calls, duvet over my head, the screen's glow flood-lighting an awning of thin white bedding, the constellations of moles on my legs charting out. On speaker-phone Hanna told me Suzann was to be cremated the next day. Suzann had been hit by a coach.

Keith says the car broke down, Hanna said. And Suzann got out to phone for help.

She got out… on the motorway? I asked.

She was alone.

Did Keith say if she had a phone or no?

She had a phone. Doesn't everyone?

And the baby?

He was with this neighbour. I met her when I called round earlier.

Fucking hell, is all I could say.

Two weeks later it's Simon's weekend to have the kids again. He had them for my training trip. He's cheesed off he has to have them again, so I don't deal with him. After we shoot the breeze, his second wife brings the kids indoors. I get a flight then head straight to Keith's. I have a bouquet of lilies, not unlike the ones Suzann sent me when my children were born, though these ones are white. Washed-out. Their cellophane rustles in my arms. My eyes prick with them. I remember Suzann's hay fever. The first thing I say to Keith when he appears at the door is, Should I pinch the pollen out of these? I'm thinking of the baby, if he has inherited her sensitivities.

Keith says, You're the only person to get flowers, Monica. Everyone's been asking, Is it donations in lieu of flowers? I mean, where would the donations go?

My taxi leaves. Behind Keith, in the lounge, the baby crab-crawls in his walker. I see two bowed legs. When he turns I see the face that goes with them, more handsome than the sum of his parents. Don't start lecturing me about putting him in that, Keith says softly.

I wouldn't dream of it, I say. I enter the lounge, crouch to better look at the child.

Come meet the boy, Keith says even though I am already there.

I turn, look back toward him. Oh, Keith, I'm so sorry. I blub. I'm mortified by it. It doesn't mortify Keith. He must be used to emotional women treating him and his boy like they are pitiful articles.

It's okay, Monica. We really are okay, you know.

The boy, nine months old, smiles at us through his translucent brown eyes. They are like his mother's and his father's. He thumps himself with a fat forearm, hides these eyes from me.

But how are you going to cope... alone? I ask.

I'm not alone. Keith smiles ever so slightly.

I stand up, blow my nose. You're absolutely right. You *will* be fine. You both will, I say.

Keith puts his hand out. I remove my coat and give it to him. He goes to hang it on the stand in the hall.

I get a lot of help, really. It's still relatively fresh, he calls like he has everything figured out. You have kids yourself, don't you? Keith asks me even though he met them when they were little. Numerous times, as it goes, when I came home to live with my mother after Simon went at me with the D-word and lawyers, Keith would have arrived home to me and my children, one crawling on this (now) old rug, one traipsing the wooden floor littered with wooden blocks and a changing mat. Somewhere a shitty nappy would be festering. Keith would stay in the kitchen, or upstairs until I had packed my family up and left.

Suzann was always happy for the mess. She loved my kids, in person, at that stage when we were the negative of the image she had of us. It was my happy, fruitful life in London that she resented. When I was struggling and lost, and couldn't enjoy what I had, Suzann was delighted to spread this tableau across her pristine lounge. It's funny how Keith forgets that I have children. Or funny how he pretends. Or, not funny at all.

I've two kids — same two — getting big now, I say.

Where are they? Are the kids back in... where is it? Keith asks.

He has been there too. He and Suzann stayed for a weekend in better days. Suzann was sick with jealousy when she heard me throwing up my breakfast. But that was pre-kids, when Simon and I lived in a better home than either of us do now. It is still not a patch on this place.

Do you mean London? I say and Keith nods. The kids are with their dad, and mummy number two. I laugh but Keith doesn't. I want to shake him for trying to hurt me this way. I say, I can't believe I missed Suzann's... I can't even say it.

The funeral, Keith says.

There is a photo of her on the table. Suzann was the type of woman who went through phases of being striking, she was in a good stage when that photo was taken. She must have liked herself in it. I'm guessing it was two years ago.

How long are you over for, Monica?

Just until Monday. I'm staying at Mum's tonight, I say. I'll stay with Hanna tomorrow. I wanted to visit a grave... or something like one. Show my respects. Meet your son.

There'll be a tree next month, I think. Nothing happens quickly in the death business.

I take a good look at him since he won't look at me, Keith has filled out, those goofy features seem less awkward. He suits middle-age better than teen-age.

Sorry, Monica! Keith snaps. I need to offer you something.

I say I'll take a coffee. I sit on the rug and pull the boy over to me by the tray of his walker. He has been eating a biscuit, drinking milk, granules of this mishmash have dribbled out his mouth and dried in. There are splats like bird poo on the cream plastic. They are on his bib too. The bib is on back to front, soft side out. I take it off him and wipe his chin. The wording says: Mummy's Boy, on the inside. The bib is sapping wet, heavy with teething drool. I fold it, set it on the arm of the chair.

Can't I make those coffees? I shout. After all, I'm here to help you.

Keith is at the door, the kettle brewing in the next room. In that case, he says, I'll have a proper drink. That alright?

You do that, I say. I'll keep an eye on the little guy.

He brings the drinks in, Keith's hand shakes as he gives me my glass. It is not coffee. It is gin and tonic. He has one too. Well, neither of us is driving, he says.

Just operating heavy machinery, I reply.

I notice his eyes have dark pockets of skin underneath. He looks older than his age. Our age. Keith will probably even out. Someday grief might suit him too.

We don't clink glasses but we sit, like I'll do tomorrow at Hanna's. Same thing.

The baby rubs his eyes. He is tired now. Keith eases himself onto the floor and makes some silly faces that make the boy smile. You can tell the boy doesn't want to smile. His eyes are red and watering. He sings MamaMamaMama. We pretend we can't hear it, like it doesn't mean a thing. Like it isn't the saddest song in the world.

So! Keith startles both me and the boy. You said your ex remarried…

I ask if I can take the boy out for a cuddle. Keith tells me to be his guest. So I cuddle him for a while. The boy resists at first. Or tries to. I can tell he is making strange, or that he would any other time only he is tired and hungry and willing to take comfort anywhere he can find it. Maybe it's my hair. Not unlike Suzann's. Long and straight. Blonde since I dyed it. Keith doesn't mention it. He usually says, You change your hair every time I see you, Monica! But not this time. Keith hands me a bottle of milk.

Does it annoy you? he asks.

I get the boy in the crook of my arm. He snatches the teat between his teeth, he sucks and sucks. His eyes get even redder. Even waterier. More translucent. He stares into mine with a look of sleep and fulfilment. A look of submission I miss. I don't know I've missed that look until I see it again, in Suzann's boy's eyes. It fractures me. My bones go soft. My heart, heavy. By this time, of examining his face, I have forgotten that Keith has asked me something. His voice, instead, is something *over there*. He does not need my attention.

Sorry, Keith, you were saying…

Simon. Keith has the decency to acknowledge my ex-husband's name, which is more decency than I allow myself to have. Keith is warming, remembering which drink I prefer. Maybe it's enough.

Simon remarried quickly.

They were roofed in and watertight within a year. After formalities.

Doesn't it annoy you?

Not anymore, I say.

He's been married to her longer than he was ever married to you, is that right?

No. So does that mean I'm the winner? I grin.

Keith laughs. Yes, you win alright. He starts to smooth out the boy's hair from crown to forehead. There is just a sprinkling of it. Blond and fine. I imagine that keeping each strand apart are the teeth marks of a comb. Anyone on the horizon? he asks. I mean, do you think that you'll remarry too?

Maybe. If I was to meet someone who's good with the kids.

Keith smiles. If you met a Mary Poppins type?

Mary: a woman's name. I wonder if I must be gay. Hanna and I have our alliance. Keith is now without his. I recall an old email from Suzann, were, in it, she referenced Keith calling Hanna's ex, Julie, a *chapstick lesbian*. Not *lipstick* enough for him.

Mark Poppins, maybe… I go quiet.

Keith takes a gulp from his glass. He says, You can't be with some-one *just because* they're good with your kids. I hear the refrain of our teenage years, Keith going: Suzann, you're so gullible! Hanna, you big whore! Monica, you're such a prick-tease!

Yeah, you're right, Keith, I admit, but you also can't be with some-one who *isn't* good with your kids. *You'll see*, is right there, right on the tip of my tongue.

Suzann's baby is asleep now. Do they still need burped at this age? I try to prop him up so he can get out of him what he needs to.

You have to make yourself happy, Keith says, lips disappearing into his mouth. He adds, Life is short.

Amen to that, brother, I say. So, how long were *you* married? The tense of my question draws a line under their life together.

Sixteen *wonderful* years.

Wow! That long! You're definitely the real winner then.

Yep, definitely won that one, he says before necking his drink. Keith sits forward. Another?

I sip, careful to let the condensation drip onto my trouser leg, not on the boy.

Go on! Sure you're a long time dead, Keith says.

I hope the night is not going to be beaded like this. Listen, Keith,

I say, take this drink. I'll stay a few hours. Put the boy to bed for you.

So we order takeaway. We are told it is a Saturday night and we will have to wait. The boy stirs from his milk-induced half-sleep griping with wind. I walk the rug with him. I kick my shoes behind the sofa. The boy spews, I'm alarmed by this because mine were not sickly babies. I put him into his sleep suit then he stays awake. He is watching me, watching Keith, watching the sinking level of his glass. Time comes for the bedtime bottle. This is a less frenzied feed. The boy is a long, languorous spread across my lap. The weight of him seeps. The heat of him moist. The boy drifts, totally unguarded, accepting of me. I still have it. He accepts the rubber teat, though not as easily, as greedily as before.

I ask Keith if Suzann was breastfeeding. Keith laughs loudly. The baby jumps. He twitches then hushes like the slow movements in a concerto. There is a dialogue between his actions. I remember Suzann playing clarinet for the school orchestra in her cerulean blue school jumper. Soft headnods. How she dotted each note with an eyeblink, like they were sneezes. Lips pursed, just like her son's are now.

Mind your own business, Keith says.

I say, Pardon me?

Suzann hated being asked that, Keith explains. She said that once she was pregnant she felt like public property.

Oh, okay, I say.

I certainly remember her non-pregnancy being public property.

One day, Keith starts, his face illuminating, This older woman... we were in a café, she saw me take the bottle from the bag and feed the boy with it. She said to Suzann, Excuse me, but in my day we believed that breast was best. Can you believe that, the nerve!

His face! He finds this story side-splittingly funny. His laugh is noiseless.

That's just nostalgia, I say. Rose-tinted. What did Suzann say?

Absolutely nothing, Keith says. Later, at home, she said, Do you know what I should have said to her? I should have said there was breast milk in the bottle. I asked her why would it be anyone's business, either way. Suzann said, You're right, Keith. In future when people ask if I'm breastfeeding I'm going to just say, Mind your own business.

Cafes are funny places though, aren't they? I say. I start to tell Keith this story about how I was once tandem feeding in a café when I got asked to cover up.

Keith rolls his eyes. Should have known you're one of those, he says.

One of what?

Did Simple Simon ever get a look in? Keith doesn't wait for me to work out if he means *a look in at me* or *a look in at our children.* Alright then, which way were you doing it? he asks.

Erm, usual way...

No. I mean discrete? Or, you know, full tit out? In your case, both tits out!

Oh, over or under, you mean?

He nods.

Does it matter?

It doesn't matter a damn to me, but it matters to people like you.

People *like me*? What does that mean?

It's like...a PhD, he says.

Now you've lost me completely.

He unloads a sigh. Take a look at Hanna, Keith says. She's always shoehorning in that she's a doctor.

No she's not!

Yes, she is, Mon! Alright, this one night we were at hers and Suzann took a bug. She was locked up in the toilet, couldn't get her to leave. Well, all I got out of Hanna was that her and that girlfriend of hers, Julie, were two doctors, so Suzann would be okay.

Hanna's a doctor of history. Julie is a doc of... I can't remember, but it's not medicine.

Exactly! So what were they going to do, tell her the year some civil war started while Suzann had it coming out both ends? Keith closes his eyes.

I think you have it coming out both ends, to be honest, Keith, I say.

Ah, never worry, it's just... self-importance. Mon, do you know I've never been anywhere where people talk about their education? Unless they have a PhD, that is. I've never had a woman talk to me about her baby. Never, Mon — at this point I feel like interjecting, Because you were probably hiding in the drinks cabinet, Keith — but they're quick to talk about how long they breastfed for. Why do we need to know? You're all so fucking wonderful because you're martyrs. He changes key, smiles shyly. Anyway, parenthood... all it is, is a competition.

It shouldn't be, I say. Okay, I accept that sometimes it feels that way. But then, Keith, so is marriage.

Yes! Keith smiles at me. And you called yourself a winner earlier.

I recall calling you the real winner.

No, marriage isn't a competition, he says. You're wrong there, Mon. Marriage is a race. And Suzann was determined to beat you.

The front door opens. All suction goes. You can feel cold air churn its way inside. You can hear the traffic boil. In with it comes a voice. Without seeing the source it sounds artificial. Hello, boys, the source calls. I turn to see her. She's forty-plus. Heavy-chested, her face thickly made-up. She stops in her tracks as though someone has walked smack into her. Her eyebrows lift, as do the corners of her mouth. I have the boy against me now, dreaming. Blowing soft raspberries against my shirt. Now he is smiling out of one side of his mouth, his little chest bubbling with huffs of laughter.

Keith leans forward on the sofa, pushes his fingers into the back of his shoe. Ruth, he says to the woman, this is Suzann's oldest friend, Mon.

Not sure I like that *oldest* part, I say, looking up at her. I move forward too, pivot myself under and around the boy.

Hello. Ruth is cool. Don't get up, you'll wake him, she tells me. To

Keith she says, I didn't know you were having company.

Just Mon, he says, she couldn't make the funeral.

I was in Vegas when I heard. It was work, not pleasure, I say.

Oh, right. That's you, is it? Ruth says.

Ruth's a neighbour of ours. Of mine, Keith corrects himself.

I get it. I know what Keith means is that she is a neighbour of his and Suzann's. *Ours* still applies. Ours now means belonging to him and the boy.

A neighbour and a good friend, Ruth says. She stands over us as if she is waiting for something, for me to leave or Keith to take her into another room. Stay, Keith tells her, we're waiting for some Chinese food.

No, thanks, Ruth says. Look, Keith, why don't I take the little man so he can sleep in a bed instead of on this woman's knee, on the floor? She is looking at the drink in Keith's hand when she says this.

If you're sure. This is how easily he accepts help. Maybe that's all it would have taken for me in London. Maybe I didn't need to return to my mother's but just hand over the kids to a neighbour: *If you're sure. Let me fetch you a bottle of cow's milk, like it's animals we are dealing with here.*

Ruth goes upstairs and scratches about, she returns with a bag and a blanket. Ten o'clock in the morning okay? she asks. Keith tells her ten o'clock is no problem. He makes it sound as though he is doing her the good turn. We parcel the boy up and she puts him in his pram still asleep. I help her down the front step. Ruth smiles her thanks. Tight and insincere. The takeaway delivery man arrives as she and the boy are leaving. I square him up and we go into the kitchen to dish out. Keith pours two gin and tonics. We take our plates, our glasses into the dining room.

Without the boy, conversation stops. Simon and I had nothing to talk about on our first meals out après-kids. What was there before them? We'd forgotten how to speak *us*. Keith and I have more history, in a way: our teen years, summers, Christmas/New Years. We have decades. A little, often. But suddenly, or maybe not suddenly at all, the past is swallowed up by the lives we are living now.

So, kids, Keith reverts. You guys had IVF too, didn't you?

You want to talk about IVF, I say. That's rich! I pick at my food, I cannot drink and eat. We've waited too long. The decision has been made. I'm going to drink. I'm going to catch Keith up. Nipples are off limits, I say, but the plumbing is... absolutely fine?

Fair dos. Keith twists his fork into noodles and starts to eat, dabbing his mouth with a black paper napkin.

It feels strange talking to a man about conception. Keith is not a doctor, as he reminds me. He is also no longer asexual and overtly-angular. Besides, these days an interest in anything intimate seems like a pathway for men. I find I can't just be interested. I'm a *single* woman.

So, is Hanna still a lesbian these days? he says through a cut of a smile. Unexpectedly there is a resemblance to the sleeping boy.

I don't think she'd say she's anything... in particular, I say. It's the *person* Hanna sees, isn't it? Not the gender. Anyway, isn't she sort of seeing a guy from work now?

Keith laughs out of his nose.

Anyway, *Keith*, I say, we never... I never had IVF. Didn't need it. You see, just when we were about to start...

Bingo!

Bingo, indeed.

But you weren't married long enough to be going down that route. Jumping the gun a bit, weren't you? he says.

I say, So, one has to be married to procreate, is that it? Keith, you've just stepped decades back in time.

Mon, I wish I could. His eyes are glazed. I used to envy your casualties, he says. That's the wrong word! I mean, casual*ness*.

Which casual*ness* is this? I ask.

Any boyfriend you had, you never wanted much from. You moved on easily. Didn't get tangled in some deep shite, unlike some girls.

Unlike whom?

Say... Hanna.

Hanna?

She'd start seeing someone and we wouldn't see her for months.

Yes, she was intense, I say. Wouldn't come up for air.

You were different though.

Maybe the other parties were more casual than I was. Ever think about that?

What do you mean?

Simon replaced me.

Oh, forget I said anything!

Suzann gave up on me, too, I say.

Don't talk soft! Keith says, Well, I'd have preferred what you had.

I drink and he eats, we evade each other's eyes. Afterwards Keith takes a packet of cigarettes from his pocket. Before you say anything, he says, I *will* open the windows after, and I *never* smoke indoors when the little guy is about. Alright?

And we are back to kids, because everything begins with them, and they don't even know it.

I thought you were only a social smoker, I say.

What's this, if not being sociable? Keith asks.

Sociable? Sure I'm just Mon. I fake a smile

Keith laughs. We clear our plates into the rubbish disposal, pour one drink, then another. By the end of the night we are lying on the rug propped up by cushions. We are *not* watching some 70s large collared cop drama on the telly, nor are we listening to the script with its flecks of misogyny. I am watching the woman in the corner of the box as she composes her sign language. I say, I didn't need IVF because they do this preliminary test before you start, and... lo and behold.

Yeah, up the pole. You already said.

Up the pole, indeed.

I am smoking now too, being sociable, watching this *corner woman* with her animated facial expressions, as she attempts to press the storyline into shape with her hands. I say, They say you're at your most fertile when you've just given birth. That's how baby number two, my boy, happened.

Like buses, Keith says.

More like coaches, I say. Suzann is still smiling at me from her photo. Fuck! I'm sorry, I say. She is still smiling. Now she's unoffendable.

I wonder if deaths happen like births, says Keith, in quick succession.

Why was she out of the car, Keith? I'm not expecting anything at this point.

It broke down, he says, his eyes look full but mine feel fuller. I'm out of the way of drinking and he, evidently, is not.

Didn't she have her mobile? Didn't she see the coach, or no?

Mon, Suzann wasn't in her right mind.

Whose mind was she in, then?

Keith's tongue flits from one dry white corner of his mouth to the other. She was upset, he says.

I lie on my side to see him better, head on my palm, elbow holding me up.

I told Suzann I was leaving her, he says.

Keith...

Suzann took the boy, drove up the street, bags full of his stuff: travel cot, nappies, etc. She gave him to Ruth.

What? I frown at him. I sit up, straight as it is comfortable to. Comfortable but not cosy.

Suzann told Ruth to keep him.

But why?

Because, Mon... Because! He rubs an eye.

Because that's where you were going.

Keith looks at me, he winces.

You complete fucker! You, Keith, wanted *her*? (I mean Ruth. Now, to differentiate, I point at Suzann's photo.) That woman devoted herself to you — and only you! — since she was a kid, really. And you wanted her to have to pass that Ruth woman's house every day? And what? You were going to live *there*? Was that the master-plan?

Here I say some unkind things about Ruth's manner and her appearance. In comparison I call Suzann a knockout. It's a strange, slippery word I have never used until tonight. It's a *Keith* kind of a word.

It's not about all that, Keith says, but it's Simon I hear.

What is it about then? I want to understand.

If it was about looks I would have gone for you over Suzann.

I wouldn't have had you, I say.

Hanna was better looking than the lot of you. Still is. Much better than you.

Hanna definitely wouldn't have had you.

Alright, if you say so, Keith says. He clears away our glasses. I follow. He sets his ashtray into the sink and fills it with water. He pours us both a drink from the tap. It's not like I didn't love Suzann, Mon. We were more like brother and sister by then. That's all.

You were *always* like brother and sister, I say. It is 2.30 a.m. on the kitchen clock.

Just stay, for God's sakes. There's a guest room, Keith says and he goes around the downstairs rooms, kitchen, dining room, lounge, putting windows on the latch.

My mum will be expecting me home.

You're thirty-seven years of age, Monica! he says.

In the guest room I stand looking at the walls. I know Suzann has painted them. They are not a professional job. There are many patches she has missed. The room is en-suite. You could never get a house like it in London for the money. It's all relative. There is an unopened toothbrush. The packaging is pockmarked. I picture Suzann letting the boy chew it while she shopped. To keep him sweet.

I take my shirt and trousers off. Down to a cami and knickers. I'm too tired to navigate my bra hooks. I turn off the ceiling light, there is a little nightlight I am sure never gets a break. It blisters like marmalade on a stove. I slip into bed where the sheets smell like sour milk. The perfume on the pillow is Suzann's. An hour or so later I wake, if I was ever truly asleep, my underwire cutting in. I think this is what has woken me until I see him at the door. I'm almost sitting, wrestling my bra off as he walks over. I pause. Keith gets in beside me. He smells sour and morose. It feels like he is wearing a rugby shirt. He gets on top. Sighs against my neck. He can't do anything. Keith has my hands. He lets go of one so I'll help him. I don't. Of course I don't. He is beyond help. Keith tries working himself. He is trying to feel something else. Something other than disappointment. He doesn't care what. His face is the colour of cider, even the whites of his eyes froth orange. I put my hands on his face so he'll look me in the eye. His tell me that this is a story about Hanna, that it eats him up that it was Suzann, then Ruth, now me, below him. Never her. Keith gets up and goes. I lie awake the rest of the night.

I can't leave now, I feel like Suzann wants me here.

In the morning I call a taxi from the guest room. I know Keith is awake, I can hear him sighing again. I swipe my bra from the carpet. Wash, dress. Walk down the stairs. I forget where I put my shoes. Forget I arrived in a coat.

After a sleep and a homemade meal at my mother's I visit Hanna. She pours that drink and tells me that story that, at first, seems as though it is about Suzann but really it is about Keith. It is an old film I can't remember watching until the final scene: they are having a drink, a laugh, Keith is pulling Hanna's hands over his straining crotch. She pulls away. Keith has repulsed Hanna. In turn she now repulses herself.

AND THREE THINGS BUMPED

I think of Stephen Kent and I remember the first time he ever collected me in that taxi of his. His name and number on a laminated card swinging on the rear-view mirror. You know the type of thing I'm talking about. He told me a fill from the moment I got into his car at the airport pick-up zone: Stephen had been a *transplant* in Chelsea until he'd come back home where, all over the province, he bought houses as investments, apart from the one he was renovating for his family. Sitting good-naturedly in Friday dinner-time traffic, he'd boasted his wife was living with her parents until the new homestead was shipshape. Stephen used to work in stocks, making money from money. Back then I toyed with writing: making something from nothing or stories from stories. I suppose there are more than two ways of looking at the one thing.

Outside my home he said, That's a nice wee house you have there.

Cheers, I said, about to leave.

Stephen said, This place is overrun with kids. How many have you got yourself?

One, I told him, and one on the way.

He turned the radio off completely. I've three, he said, two lads and a girl. He sat back so he was looking at me full on in the rear-view mirror. He was somewhere between a pair of eyes and a hard thick neck. You have to give stuff up when kids are involved, don't you? Stephen said.

We only had our daughter then so I couldn't tell if that would catch us up. Trudy and I didn't stop each other doing the things we loved. I thought about her and her surfing, and me and my writing. Stephen and I got talking and lost track of time. Trudy looked out the living room window at us.

Someone wants you home, Stephen said though neither of us moved.

Trudy's easygoing, I told him.

That's good, he said. Then you're a lucky man.

Stephen told me his neighbours were young guys. They invited him to the bar, coaxed him into going to Ravenhill to watch the rugby. Stephen normally ended up driving. He said sometimes he felt they used him for lifts. There was never any point in leaving the Merc at home, which was the car he drove when he wasn't taxiing, and he didn't charge them. They're not a bad crowd, he told me. It's good to have the company of young fellas.

Stephen had a decade on me. Just had his fortieth. He had a thing for numbers which I understood as being residual from his broker days. He talked about being born on the tenth of May, that his daughter had the same birthday. He was one of ten kids.

I think ten might be my lucky number, he said.

I listened quite easily. Always thirsty for a story back then. He elaborated on his living arrangements, admitting he and his wife were on a trial separation he believed they'd reconcile from, especially once she saw this house he was building for her and the children: whom I recall were seven and nine and ten, or thereabouts.

I said, Forgive my nosiness but is there anyone else in the picture?

No, none of that, Stephen told me. He was still wearing his

wedding ring. I'll tell you something, he said, and it goes no further. In my experience money is the killer. People can put up with all sorts. Cheating would never do the damage money does.

So let me get this straight, I said, it's having too much money that ruins things?

He squinted in the mirror at me. Money is the killer, he repeated. It always has been with me and the missus. She wanted me to come back here so she could be near the grandparents for babysitting. She said she was lonely in Chelsea. All those millions of people and she couldn't find one she liked! We used to holiday in Dubai. New York. You sacrifice things, don't you? The house you want, the motors. I came back for her and what happened? If I'm being honest—and what's the point in not being—she was a very selfish person. What she put me through—and I'll not get into it all—but there aren't many men who would put up with the things that I put up with. In the end I couldn't anymore.

Yes, you can't be doing with that, I said.

He dried up, so I told him it had been good talking to him. Stephen turned side on and shook my hand. He liked the look of the cufflinks Trudy had bought me: two silver crowns with little jewels set into the spikes. They were flash for my taste. A gift for my thirtieth I didn't have long. I lost one in the airport after a month or two. Trudy never really forgave me. One is, after all, sort of jobless on its own.

Stephen knew they were Westwood, who, as it turned out, was the only designer Stephen wore when he lived in Chelsea. Then out of nowhere he said, My wife did time. You asked so I'm going to tell you. She did time for fraud. Was stealing from me the whole time, and from her employer.

Jesus, I said and sat back, what else could I do?

Ruth, he said, that's her name. When Ruth came to Chelsea she got a job for the Crown Prosecution Service, started writing dodgy receipts. I just couldn't live with a woman like that, not in my profession. If you really want to know, I had to leave the market. I was warned it could have repercussions on me. They did me a severance deal and I took it. I'd be a tool not to. Ruth comes from a family… well, let's just say they aren't short of a bob or two, so between them and me the kids are kept right, you know? And Ruth too. And I don't want you to think that I wish her ill, because I don't.

No of course not, I said.

But if I wasn't a gentleman I could tell you a few things, said Stephen.

How long did she do?

Where? Inside? Not long. He rubbed his eye. A good solicitor, if you ever need one, is all you need. Remember that, pal. If you ever find yourself on the wrong side of the law, a shit-hot solicitor will seal the deal. And keep your mouth shut. It does you no good if you can't hold your water, do you know what I'm saying?

I presume you get what you pay for, I said. In terms of legal representation. Same as everything.

Absolutely, he nodded. It is the same as everything. Especially in money issues. A good solicitor will talk it all around and before you know it, you don't know what end of you is up. Well, Joe Bloggs, doesn't know. People who aren't used to money chat. It has its own language. I don't need to be doing this, I live in a real nice place, nice but small, I like working with people. You couldn't beat it really. He yawned. Look, it's been good talking to you but I have to get back now, the kids will be calling me. I like to tell them I love them every day. Even days I don't see them. Make sure you do that too. Especially when the next one comes along, Stephen added letting me know he had been listening. Don't let the wee child feel left out. It's not a nice thing. I'm saying this as the eldest of a large family. And you're on the right tracks too, going away to do your own thing, maybe me and Ruth should have done more of that. You get out of the way of it. Don't end up like us.

Okay, I said and we re-enacted our handshake.

They are nice cufflinks, he said, nearly longingly and he turned to put his hands back on the wheel.

They are quite nice, I said and I finally got out.

He was some talker, I said. Trudy shook her head and said she'd made something in the restaurant and there was plenty of it left in the fridge.

That night we lay in bed discussing Stephen. She was sceptical, like I had been, like anyone would be. Why would he be taxiing if he's so loaded? she asked.

He turned the meter off all that time we were sat outside.

I should hope so too.

He did say something good, that we should never stop doing the things we love.

Well then, Trudy said, maybe he was worth listening to.

*

We put ourselves aside for a couple of years. It happens, even though you vow it won't. Having a kid is a whirlwind. The house needed doing up. That fell by the wayside too. We slept together once, maybe twice a month, if we weren't exhausted. Having a second child was twice the work. It makes sense but somehow I hadn't bargained on it. At times it seemed we might crack.

We went to Paris for a weekend. Trudy's dad minded the kids. He hadn't a clue, poor man. Their clothes hadn't even been unpacked when we returned. God knows what he was doing. Potty training the youngest had to start all over again, but at least we got away. We had a good time but it felt cultural, like a school trip. Our feet were worn to the bone with all the walking, then we fell asleep watching the show at the Moulin Rouge.

A week after we came home we spoke about it, how we should have been unable to keep our hands off each other, in Paris of all places. We wondered aloud if we were done. And what we would do with the house. How would we tell the kids? It happened in a blink.

I looked at Trudy and she looked at me and started crying, saying we were like passing ships. I'm so busy I'm meeting myself at the front door, she said. I'm going to miss you so much.

It struck me how ridiculous we were being, how easily we were prepared to tear our little family apart. I don't want this, I told her.

Nor do I, she said in a heavy wet voice. You're my favourite person in the world. All our friends always say we're perfect for each other and we are.

It was then Stephen came into my head, and everyone else I knew who had split up with their partners, especially where kids were involved, and I knew Trudy and I could hold it together. I told her she should go back to surfing and I should go back to writing. It would mean that our time together would be less, but quality.

*

It must have been five years on, I was coming home from a writing retreat and Trudy had the car. She needed it because she was working nine to five. The kids were both at school by then and we had finally found a good design in the way we lived. We were at a good stage. The kids liked to learn and you could have conversations with them. And me and Trudy laughed together lots. It was then we were at our happiest, together and with the kids, but then I wondered, because we never *really* spoke, what was on her mind. We were like colleagues, in the many revolutions our relationship had taken. Although we were connected more in bed, but it was all a bit predictable. Then once in a while we would have a mind-blowing night and my head would ease for another while.

I got a bit jealous of Trudy's new happiness, I have to admit. She was working in the prisons and I'd expected her to hate it, but she was getting something emotionally that we didn't seem to need from each other anymore. I was working too, and writing, but it wasn't really going anywhere. I wasn't putting myself out there. Wasn't seeking publication. Something always held me back.

When Stephen collected me he asked about the retreat. I told him about the lake, how you walked around it for inspiration, how it was peaceful but I wanted to write strong stuff that really was the opposite of how it had been there.

But you did get peace and quiet to do it?

I did, I said.

His name card was stuck to the dash now and it had a photo. I could see his face but still his eyes flitted to me in the mirror. He was driving another heap of junk, working for a company instead of for himself. The radio kept coming through, telling him and his colleagues where to go next. Stephen lowered the volume.

I haven't seen you around in ages, I said to him.

He looked at me in the mirror. His hard thick neck tensed. I realised I wouldn't know him out on the street. You gave me a lift in the past, I said. You were going through some things back then.

Like what, he said.

You were maybe splitting up with your wife, pal, I said.

That's right, he said but Stephen was chary. How are you doing, pal?

Not bad, I said.

And what about this writing? Are you writing a book?

I am, I said. Been writing it for years. I'm blocked.

Ah, he said. I have a story for you. You can have it if you want.

It's about a woman who ended up in jail for stealing money from her employer and wrangled her way out of the conviction. You'll sell millions of copies.

He had no memory of me. Had probably told this story thousands of times since I'd last been in his cab. Instead of letting him think I'd spent all that time mulling it over, I pretended I'd never heard it.

Is this a real story?

It's real alright. It's my ex I'm talking about. She spent time inside, got the conviction turned over, came out and got it fixed on another poor fucker.

Jesus, that's mad, I said.

Are you married? he wanted to know first.

Practically. A very long term relationship, I said.

You'd never believe what they'd do to you. Honest to god, you just never know.

Sounds terrible.

I was living in London, he said. I met this girl on the net, Ruth, and I left there to be with her. She already had three kids. Two lads and one girl. All different dads: that should say it all! I came over here to be with her. She was cute. I'll give her that. Nice little shape to her. I talked her into moving back to London with me. We left the kids with her parents for a while to give things a go. The plan was they were going to come over too. Listen to this for coincidence, her daughter's birthday was on the same day as mine. Tenth of May, he said. I'm one of ten kids and Ruth lived in 10 Gorse Lane. You know, you have to listen to all these signs when they're as powerful as that.

Absolutely you do!

I had my own business over there, a taxi firm — he had excluded the stock broker line — and she was bored so I encouraged her to get out and work. We walked into a registry office one day and got married.

Weren't your family annoyed to have missed out?

Ah, no, I've been married before. They're not bothered. My

mother never liked Ruth anyway.

Why not?

All the kids.

He pulled up into town. Fuck sake, there's an accident up ahead, he said. I'm going to have to turn and go back the long way, that okay with you, pal? I'll cut the meter here sure.

He'd become impatient like the rest of them.

I appreciate it, I said.

I took those kids on like my own, you know. I told everyone they were mine. Now they won't even see me. You got any? he asked.

Two, I said. Seven and five years old. My girlfriend was expecting the little one the last time I was in your cab.

I wouldn't remember that, he laughed. God knows how many fares I've had in here in the meantime.

I'm sure, I said.

Ruth hated London. I had a good job over there, making good money, a fleet of motors, holidays to Dubai. The money was unbelievable. It would shock you. I got a bit materialistic, I'm not afraid to say. We were taking out loans and living like king and queen, then it turned out she was being sly.

How so?

Writing fake invoices. Saying they were from court witnesses using my cabs. The cash was going into an account she'd set up. She was using fake names, the lot. She got time and wormed her way out of it. By that time we were back here, and me left with nothing. The shirt on my back and little else. Think how ashamed I was to go to my mother and tell her she was right all along.

Sure you can't help who you fall for, I said. You were decent, taking on her kids and giving them that lifestyle.

He frowned. Yes, he said. Then the bitch got out of it because the taxi firm was mine. She framed me.

God, what happened then?

I had to do time, didn't I! Stitched up like a kipper, you know.

Million quid scam. They couldn't account for the whole of it.

That's awful!

He nodded, he pulled into my street.

How long did you get?

Six years, out in three. It's shocking what someone you once loved and trusted can do to you. I hope you have better joy with your missus.

Just over here, I said and he pulled up.

I recognise this house now, he said and he looked it over. Your fascia, he said, don't you find that a ball-ache?

What's that, I said getting my wallet out of my back pocket.

The wood. Wouldn't you be better getting the uPVC? You don't have to maintain it, it's just…you paint that, and then in between being arsed, it looks like shite, you know?

I bit my tongue. There you go, hold on to the change, I said.

No, no, he said and searched for a few coins, his hard thick neck tensing.

Trudy was ready to head out to the water, just for a walk. I told her about the accident and she said she'd leave the car at home. Do you remember I met this taxi driver years ago? I asked her. She didn't. Well, he was giving me a lift there and he was saying he'd been framed for fraud.

They're all framed, she said.

He got six years and now he blames the wife.

Don't you all, Trudy said and she grabbed her coat and left without so much as a kiss on the cheek, shouting back that she'd be an hour or two.

The kids were outside on the trampoline. There was a net surround but the zip never worked from the get-go. I made myself a salad and ate it at the window, waving out to them.

The girl came in straight away. Did you write your book, Daddy?

I wrote a bit of it, I said kissing her on the top of the head. The boy soared out, hitting his head on the corner of the boiler house. It was only a nick but it was deep. Holding a cloth to his head I tried calling Trudy. Her phone laughed like church bells on the counter.

I got the kids in the car and we're heading to A&E. I forgot about the tail-backs in town. They were moving the bashed-up car. There was an ambulance at the side of the road, a woman in her seventies sitting with a blanket and paramedics around her.

Trudy, where are you? I said, thinking we might pass her.

You should have left a note, Daddy, my daughter said.

We'll be home in no time, I said.

Once we got to the hospital I managed to get through to Trudy at home. I'm taking a taxi, she said.

I told her it was a waste of cash, that it was a small hole and we were getting seen next.

Okay, she said, sounding emptied.

We were at the hospital for three hours. They put glue in his head and gave him stickers.

What happened here? the doctor asked my daughter.

I noticed the bruise under her eye. What did happen to you? I asked.

A boy in class hit me, she said.

I've been away, I explained. I was only in through the door and my partner had to go out. She never said. She left her phone behind. What did the teacher say? Did you tell your mother?

She looked at the floor.

Why did this boy hit you? I asked her.

I don't know, she said.

I bet he likes you, said the doctor giving her a sticker too.

I sent the kids ahead, told them to wait at the main door. I said to the doctor, I hope you aren't treating my daughter when she's older because some boyfriend is knocking her about.

He looked at me singularly. I wanted to say more but I let it drop.

At home Trudy came out to meet us in the driveway, she lifted our son into the house. Come here till I see my brave soldier.

The boy sat with us past bedtime to make sure he wasn't concussed. Trudy put our girl to bed and met me in the kitchen. I think it was an accident, Trudy whispered, but I'll go and talk to her teacher tomorrow. I'll find out more. I'm sorry I left my phone here.

It's almost like you didn't want to be found.

I didn't know that would happen.

They're still young, I said. They still need us a lot.

We all still need each other, Trudy said.

And that is what we proceeded to do for the next five years, pull apart and come together. The kids grew. They didn't need us much at all. It was a slap in the face how fast it happened.

I rarely used cabs anymore. The last time I saw Stephen I was in the back of his. Trudy and I had separate cars by then. Mine was in getting a new clutch. In his photo he'd aged a lot but his eyes looked the same. I was mindful of the fascia we'd got reconditioned. He never looked at it. We dropped my son off. Stephen watched as he walked into school.

I've three myself, he told me. All getting big now.

Yes, I said, it isn't long in happening.

I hadn't the same time for him. Only as a story, you understand. He had something bitter in him that wasn't pleasant to be around. You married? I asked him.

I was, he said, three times believe it or not.

So you're on the market?

Nah, he said, I've given up on all that. Once I had the ring on my finger I would get claustrophobic, he said. You know how it is.

But sure if you love someone, isn't it worth it?

That's not my experience.

Sure it's hard no matter who you are and what you have, and who you're with.

I'll have to take your word for it, he said. My kids were all with the last wife, Ruth. None with the other ones. Ruth doesn't let them see me anymore. Haven't seen them in years.

That's tough, I said.

You're telling me.

What age are they? (I knew they'd be adults by now.)

Hmm…(he couldn't remember.) The grandparents won't allow them to see me.

Sure isn't it up to the kids?

But the grandparents have them and they're loaded. The kids know which side their bread is buttered, don't they? Ruth's parents badmouth me in front of them.

Why's that? If you don't mind me asking.

No, I don't mind at all, said Stephen. They loaned me money to start up a taxi firm in Chelsea. They had the kids while we got sorted, then the business went belly-up and they never let off me with it.

Shit!

They fucken accused me of stealing from them, then it was investigated and they found out it was an account in Ruth's name. Their own daughter was doing the stealing.

That's awful, I said.

It was awful. To be honest, it wasn't that bad for Ruth. She got out after a while. It was someone else, someone, a business partner of ours who was really framing her.

Who was this?

I'm not going to name names.

I respect that, I said.

I was very disappointed in him. He was a tool. They put that fella away. He made a lot of mistakes but he did his time.

(Of course, I'd looked Stephen Kent up. I knew there was no taxi firm. That he and Ruth had both worked for CPS. That pride of his was so thick it was unswallowable.)

And so were you and Ruth not able to put it behind you, after?

She had someone else by then. She was always gorgeous. People would think I was her da. They'd all look at her when we were out anywhere. I'd be proud as punch.

Wouldn't you move heaven and earth to see your kids?

I have. I always had that fatherly thing about me. My parents had ten kids. I'm the oldest.

That's a lot.

I thought I'd be a dad, but just two kids, because our folks had no time for us you know. They just popped kids out. My father was a prick and my mother, she let him give her dog's abuse, you know.

You couldn't get away with that now.

No, you can't, said Stephen. My mother always hated Ruth. I found it strange when I saw the two of them as being so alike. The shit they'd put up with from men. I wanted to give Ruth and the kids everything. They didn't have much to begin... well, the kids weren't mine biologically. They were, I don't want you to think badly of her, but they had different dads.

Ah, no, sure it's not like I know her. I'm not about to judge the girl.

Ruth's parents were very tight with her, said Stephen. She really deserved a lot more than she had. We all do, if I'm honest. We should have more than our lot and not feel bad about wanting that. We give up enough, don't you think? If we ever had it to begin with. I want for nothing these days. He pulled up outside my work, scratched the side of his hard thick neck. Anyway, Ruth has someone else now. I hope he knows what a lucky bastard he is.

THE WORLD'S GETTING SMALLER
ALL THE TIME

The town's best seafood restaurant was filled to the gills with Saturday night diners. Two couples met up for a B.Y.O.B. good-bye meal: Natalie and Tab, and Charmaine and Stuart—who were to emigrate to Australia the next day. Melbourne, to be exact. The men were quiet, especially Tab. Stuart had cooled off from his earlier hyperactivity when he'd met Natalie with that hug that lifted her off the pavement outside. Charmaine told the waiter to leave her bottle of wine at their table. Forget the ice-bucket.

Remember the time we came here for Gina's hen? she asked Natalie, topping up her glass.

I remember, said Natalie.

Then we came here before, all four of us, didn't we? Before One Big Weekend?

Tab looked from his soup to Charmaine, diagonally across the table. He wiped his mouth with the back of his hand. You saying your goodbyes already? he asked her.

No, she said. Not goodbye.

Sayonara? asked Stuart, a smirk crawling across his lips. Auf Wiedersehen?

Charmaine reddened. Just asking if you all remember, that's all! She sipped her drink. Stuart gave her an affectionate, protective smile.

Natalie said, There'll be lots of great eateries in Oz, I'd imagine. Different cultures.

Melting pot, Tab said.

Stuart nodded. Yeah, sure. There'll be great grub.

Tab stood. You okay? Natalie asked him.

Getting some air, he said.

She watched him wade out, hands grabbing the backs of chairs, pulling himself forward past the queue for a table. Smaller the further he went. Tab's going to miss you both, Natalie said.

Charmaine coughed. He'll miss *him*. She nudged Stuart. Tab's never much liked me.

Yeah he has, Natalie found herself say.

Charmaine murmured something. Stuart shook his head and inhaled. I'll go see if he needs a hand, he said. Charmaine laughed at this.

Natalie watched a young waitress lift plates from the table beside theirs, place them on a huge round tray, back through the kitchen's swinging door, her face flustered and red. The waitress smiled and Natalie smiled back.

You ever waitressed? Charmaine asked.

Me? No, Natalie paused, she thought of something to add but couldn't, settled for, Have you?

No. Who wants to keep up that façade? Charmaine asked. Pretending you like people and they continually treat you like shite. She began to separate the corners of her paper napkin with her index finger and thumb.

We haven't treated her — the waitress — badly, said Natalie.

Yeah, 'course, said Charmaine. No, we wouldn't be bad customers. Some people are though.

Natalie watched the kitchen door swing again and the waiter appear this time. The diners, everybody, looked happy. You think you'll miss the town, Char? she asked.

A bit. Stuart thinks I'm being a moron, Charmaine halted at first then her speech picked up pace. After two bloody years filling in paperwork, sorting a new job and visas, now I'm saying, *You know, I'll miss the salon... my wee house.* But I'll have a new house. A new salon to work in... in a better place. Fucken sunshine! Charmaine shook her fists victoriously at the chandelier above them, closed her eyes as if it was the closest thing they had to a sun. She let out a laugh.

Natalie considered the laugh, the fidgeting, this glut of remembering. Before, everything had been for *tomorrow* with Charmaine. Always living in tomorrow till tomorrow came.

It'll be strange for you though, said Natalie, moving to somewhere you haven't even been on holiday.

That's not an issue. Stuart's brother has lived in Melbourne for years, Charmaine said.

You mean Tim?

Yeah, Tim. Know him?

Went to swim club together.

Did you?

Natalie nodded.

Tim's a fish! And the beach... He surfs too. Nat, I mean, if you went to swim club then you're a fish too. Look, why don't you come with us?

Yeah, eleven o'clock flight tomorrow morning, right? No probs! Stow me away in your suitcase.

What a sarky moo you are! I mean, in good time.

It's not really me.

Who is it then? Charmaine asked her, eyes hefty with the sulk.

No, I didn't mean... But that's the thing too. There's Libbie to think of.

Your Libbie would love Melbourne. Tim says the kids learn

outdoors, loads of sports, and parks. Wouldn't Libbie just love that!

Natalie looked at the window for a sight of the men. There was none. She said, There's Michael to consider.

But Natalie, you never married him. He has no rights. My cousin's a legal secretary, she said that couples are shooting themselves in the — I dunno, *legal foot*, is that a thing? — by *not* marrying. Anyway, that's a bad thing. But the upshot is — if you have kids, and you *aren't* married — Michael has no say over where you bring Libbie. Charmaine's mouth twisted into a vague question mark.

Still. I wouldn't take his daughter to the opposite end of the world, Natalie told her.

Really?

Of course not, she said.

Wouldn't you just love to see his face if you were to say...

I don't hate Michael, Charmaine. We were just young. Probably could've tried harder to work on things.

Tab would like Melbourne.

Natalie took a drink of water. Ice tinkled in the tall glass. What time are you heading off in the morning?

Eleven, Charmaine stopped. We're all ready for our mains here, she shouted over to the waiter who came and cleared the table, excused his busyness. Made small talk about the Saturday night offer. Tab and Stuart returned.

Enjoy your *air*? asked Charmaine.

It was buenos, muchos gracias, said Stuart.

Trying to persuade Natalie to join us in Oz, Charmaine explained. I could picture this. She swilled her wine glass in a circular motion as if she was already on a tasting in one of those vineyards she bummed about. I could see this. Us. Only by the beach.

The harbour here not good enough for you? Tab asked her, although you wouldn't have known who he was speaking to. Natalie was finding it harder to get his full attention.

Not the same, mate, Stuart stated. But you'll see that when you visit.

If I can, said Tab.

Natalie felt Charmaine's eyes on her, urging her to urge him to commit. She couldn't. Stuart took a beer from the plastic bag at his feet, slid one toward Tab. He declined it, wanting a clear head.

Look at you, Tabo, you sensible cunt. Nat, you've changed this cunt. For the better, might I add! Natalie? Stuart acquired a serious expression, began to saw his chin with his forefinger. Nat, I know I used to keep you going, saying you had him under the thumb... just saying though, it was a joke. In truth, Nat, I'm delighted someone's tamed the crazy bastard. I'll not fret about him now. Stuart stuck his tongue out, his teeth clamping it.

Natalie watched the looks on their faces, secretive and hateful. But not on Stuart's, he had a vulnerability. A sweetness. Still she allowed herself a comeback. Yeah, I mean, I never understood the *under the thumb* remarks, she said. I never stopped Tab doing anything. Never stopped him going anywhere he wanted to. She forced herself to maintain the eye contact her boyfriend couldn't, with Stuart and Charmaine, only now Tab's eyes were boring into the side of her face.

He took the beer, cracked back the ring pull then left it in front of him, an amber dribble pooling on the white tablecloth. Stu was only fucken joking you!

I know he was, Natalie whispered.

It was just that time, said Charmaine, remember we were to go to Derry together, but Tab stayed home with you instead, and we had to drive down alone? That's the time you said Tab was under the thumb. Wasn't it, babe? He *was* joking though.

Derry? Natalie asked. That was the day Libbie fell off her scooter. Tab could've gone. I did tell you, Tab, to go ahead. I said Michael was coming to sit with me while we waited for the X-ray and the hospital bed, before Libbie's op. You insisted on staying, Tab.

Stuart hiked a thumb at Charmaine. She was raging she had to stay sober and drive back.

Tab's face finally turned away from Natalie. It was a good gig?

Oh, fucken awesome, said Stuart. But when you're a family man... kiss goodbye. He kissed his palm, gave a cupped-hand wave like a child. Like Libbie at Michael's window as Natalie had driven away.

The young waitress set their meals before them. Natalie gathered herself forward to breathe in the grease from her twice-fried chips. Paprika from her calamari. At least you don't have to drive tomorrow, Natalie said. You'll be able to have those little airplane bottles of vino.

Charmaine steadily eyed her. No, I'll be fine. Watch a few movies. Be fine.

After they ate their mains, the waiter offered them the dessert menu. The women declined. The men asked for a banana split, to share. Like two boyfriends, Stuart kidded.

Fuck off, tosser, Tab told him, running his hand over his buzz cut, his hand over his face. He looked so tired.

Why are you being a bitch to your boyfriend? Charmaine asked Tab, laughing widely, showing tonsils and fillings.

Tab took a sip of his Coke. He didn't touch the beer. Did you see on the news, he said, that man in Melbourne? Killed his ex-girlfriend.

Then there was this other one, said Natalie, a dad. Bashed his own kid to death in the middle of a football field. Light of day. The place hiving.

Stuart's face creased. In Melbourne?

Yep, Tab said.

Stuart said, Tell me this now!

Then last year there was that girl, said Tab, grew up twenty minutes away. She went to the local college. She emigrated too. Remember she was walking home? Was raped. Tab put out his thumb. Beat. He added a finger. Strangled to death. Another finger.

Shut up! said Charmaine. These kinds of things can happen anywhere.

Maybe, said Tab.

Do they fuck! said Stuart.

'Course they do. Don't listen to them two, Charmaine pleaded.

Stuart fixed his collar. Hey, it's not me I'm worried about. No fucker messes with this machine. He flexed a bicep, showed the superficial scarring on his wrists.

In the car park of her gym.

What is?

The man who killed his girlfriend, said Tab. That was another one, stabbed her to death.

Fucked-up, mate.

Charmaine looked at Tab. Do you mind? We get the picture loud and clear.

The *message* loud and clear. Stuart stuck his tongue out.

Do you think I haven't heard all this scaremongering from people already? said Charmaine. My mum gets google alerts on Melbourne, tells me everything that happens in the news there. Never the good stories because they're never on the news. Just the bad ones.

She'll miss you, said Natalie, her stomach cramping.

Charmaine said, She'll visit.

Wanted to leave him, the woman in the car park, Tab said then quietened. Natalie narrowed her eyes at him.

Charmaine edged forward. But wasn't he abusive? She had an order out against him, didn't she? Knew what he was like.

She did, said Natalie. Watch your back. She straightened up, lifted her elbows off the table, nodded at the waiter holding the sweet. He placed it in the centre of the table. Everyone shuffled. Replaced their spines around the table.

Stuart placed a hand on his stomach, two fingers slipping between the buttons on his shirt, touching a ripped muscle on his abdominals. He said, I'm gonna be sitting on my ass all day tomorrow and the next day. Was this such a good idea?

He says! Charmaine jumped into the gap in the conversation, beating 200 calorie beers into him. *Now* he's worried.

It's fruit, basically, said Stuart.

You're fruit, basically! said Tab.

Natalie watched the flirtation of their bromance. The ardent brutality in their sports. Contact. Rough and tumble. Their need to spar with each other in worthless life-unaltering debates. The necessity for each other physically, whereas Natalie didn't care if, for the rest of her life, another woman never so much as linked an arm through hers.

Sure, he'll swim off his dessert, said Natalie.

That's right, said Charmaine, Natalie was saying that she used to go dipping with your Tim, Stuart.

Dipping? Tab sliced into the banana split, ate his share in two mouthfuls and sent the rest to Stuart.

Natalie tutted. Swim club… in the leisure centre.

Stuart tugged a strand of Charmaine's hair. That's right. Did I never tell you, Char?

She brushed his hand away. No. Why wouldn't you have told me that, *Stu*?

I don't know. Just thought I'd said. Stuart took up a spoon and ate the remains of the sweet.

Charmaine shrugged. Funny, she said.

What's funny about it?

Dunno.

It's good to have secrets, isn't it, Natalie? Tab was sitting back, putting his weight on two legs of the chair, stretching his arms and interlocking his hands behind his head. Secrets keep it exciting. Meetings, she thought she heard him say.

Do they?

Apparently. Tab bolted forward as if he'd received a shock from the ground, the chair rocking slightly. Then, all of a sudden, stillness.

Charmaine took it up. It's funny you thought you'd mentioned it, Stuart, she said. I mean, they were kids, I'm surprised that you remember — not remember telling me — but remember at all. Who cares? No offence, Nat.

Stuart put a hand on Charmaine's arm and tried to catch her eye. Could hardly forget it, he said, not when it was something they did for years. I'd come out of karate every Saturday and have to sit in the spectator's pews and watch for an hour, them two swimming. Every week for years. So, yeah...

You watched her in the pool, did you now? asked Tab.

She had none of all *this*, then. Stuart mimed Natalie's curves with his hands like Prince in a music video. Sorry, Natalie, I'm being a prick. I know I'm being a prick.

Natalie stood. Excuse me. I need the ladies. She felt heavy. Her tampon felt insufficient to hold all her blood and she was losing so much of it. In the toilet she remembered her clutch bag left on the table. Natalie took a pound coin from the back of her jeans and let it fall into the machine: her trolley pound.

Before she dropped Libbie to Michael's she'd taken her to the shops, bought Libbie a Disney DVD they'd already seen in the cinema together. Bought a bag of sweet and salted popcorn in the groceries. She'd stood in the kitchen while Michael filled two bowls up and she heard the start of the film, the opening song to accompany some life-changing event, usually a parent's death. The films were formulaic like that. Michael asked her when she was going to do it. Natalie lifted a glass from the cupboard and poured herself a drink of water. The sameness of everything made her teeth chatter, her stomach twist, like she could easily stay there, watch the movie, be as though she'd never left him. But there was a protocol. Something to get out of before the getting back into something. Something that fitted better. Or didn't need to fit at all. The kitchen. Glasses and bowls. Michael. It felt like Natalie was in her best makeup even though she was barefaced.

She'd kissed him, the fridge door cold at her back, stopped his hand at her waistband, explained she was on her period.

Natalie let the tampon plop into the toilet. She put her foot on the toilet seat and inserted a new one. She fixed her hair at the mirror and thought about Michael's text again: *Don't put it off. Be strong.*

She'd felt brighter as she'd loaded Tab's freezer with risottos and portions of haddock. She'd applied her makeup, straightened her hair, decided to change her top only, too bloated for her good trousers, and Charmaine never wore dresses which meant Natalie couldn't either.

Natalie had signed a *good luck on your new life* card and slipped in a hundred dollars she'd paid over the odds for, with the bank closing early on Saturdays, and the travel agent's piss-taking commission.

Tab hadn't asked her to sign it on his behalf but unquestionably she had. Maybe she was paying Stuart to be there for Tab after, in one form or another. He would need a friend.

Natalie set down the stairs, the restaurant pounding. The place was full with people Natalie either recognised or knew, only they had taken on a different shade, turned into strange nocturnal animals buzzing with life and small in-house dance steps. She would happily stay here. Happily have Libbie fly the nest. Be content that she would always return to her and Michael. They would never leave.

Stuart was paying the bill. Natalie was looking at their table, looking for her bag, when Stuart cuffed her wrist with his hand and said, I know what you're looking for, but this is our treat. Sorry if I embarrassed you there, he uttered.

Natalie felt better about her generosity. She felt better for Tab's meanness. Her bag was away, in Tab's hand. The good luck card held by the slightest grip of Charmaine's fingers. She still hadn't opened it. Charmaine let the card swing, one hand on Tab's shoulder as she leant forward, slightly tiptoed to talk to him. Then they fell away from each other, Charmaine smiling afresh and shuffling in her heels to join Stuart in the doorway. He held the door for them all. Tab pushed Natalie's clutch bag at her chest, the cold gumminess of the leather sticky on the small v of her cleavage.

You'll be fine, Charmaine shouted back to Tab, then to Natalie an explanatory, He's gonna miss his boyfriend.

Now the card was gone. Natalie looked at Charmaine's bag, the paper corner stood from a mid-pulled zip. Natalie hoped she wouldn't forget about it. She'd feel cheap to alert her there was money inside. Oh, you've got your card from Tab and I, she said and swore she saw Tab sneer at her.

They walked down the back streets to Charmaine and Stuart's home. Here, Tabo, Stuart said, remember we chased Bill and Ben the wank-stain men up here? Gave them a right good hiding.

Who's reminiscing now, soppy twats? said Charmaine falling back to realign the pairs, so the men walked together and she walked with Natalie.

The air was crisp. Noses, fingers and toes were nipped with it by the time they reached the house. Music blared. People hugged Charmaine and Stuart to them as they came through the door. Charmaine's mum shouting, Here they are! Here they are! They're all here. Like they, all four for them, were leaving.

There was a *good luck* banner pulled taut across the arch of where the living room met the dining area, a plastic horseshoe on the coffee table, an arrangement of spirit bottles forming a crescent around it. A couple of fellas wore Aussie hats complete with swinging corks, giving it all the *G'day, Bruces* and *G'day, Sheilas.*

Charmaine's mum made her way to Natalie. What can I get you to drink, love?

I'm driving.

You get parked out there?

No, just left the car by the harbour. Sure it's not far.

You won't be wanting to walk back for it later. Get a Joe Baxi or leave it till tomorrow, have a wee wine.

No, ta. I can't really drink.

Alco-pop then?

No, seriously.

You preggers?

Tab's face twitched. Keep your voice down, she's not fucken pregnant.

Natalie watched as he crossed over to meet a friend. They pumped fists.

I've not got a great stomach for drink, to tell the truth, Natalie said.

I've a bad stomach too and I'm getting pissed, Charmaine's mum told her. You'll just think we're all mad if you're the only one sober.

Don't be silly! I've to collect my daughter from her dad's tomorrow. I don't want to be suffering. Natalie was aware of Tab in her peripheral, his reflection in the silver-framed mirror on top of the fireplace. He was listening to the fella but watching her and Charmaine's mum.

What age is the child now?

Three, said Natalie.

Well, fucken cherish her! My wee girl is twenty-two and going to the furthest away part of the planet tomorrow. Prob'ly never see her again.

You will! The world's getting smaller all the time. There're texts now. And video chats.

You're a mum, 'magine your wee girl away.

Natalie squeezed her hand. They might not even like it, she said. The grass isn't *always* greener.

Charmaine's mum locked her in an embrace. Started to sob into Natalie's neck. Natalie held her like that, rubbed her back for a minute or so then left for the kitchen and better light: an escape from the music she could feel beat inside her chest. She thought of Libbie in her proper bedroom, how she had been living in two opposite ends of the earth already. Now she was where she should always have been. There had already been the weekly drip of her belongings back to Michael's to make tomorrow easier.

Natalie fished her phone from her clutch. *Call me, if you want to.* Michael's text was anxious. Excited. He wanted to talk to her. Today of all days he hadn't wanted to let her go.

Who's that from? Tab asked from behind her.

Just checking an email.

He took a bottle of Corona from the ice-filled washing basin in the sink. Beheaded it against the counter with the heel of his hand. Tab swiped a lime from the bowl. Anything interesting? he asked. He pulled the drawers out.

They're leaving a lot of stuff, don't you think? Natalie asked.

Charmaine's ma can use it, sure. She's taking over the lease, getting out of the housing exec.

Oh, okay.

Surprised she didn't tell you. Looked as thick as thieves just there now.

I feel bad for her... being left.

Why? She's one bitch-cunt!

Natalie deleted Michael's thread of texts. She put her phone away. Why do you say that? she asked.

Tab carved the lime up. He tipped the slices from the board back into the bowl. Lime juice bubbled on the side of the blade. He said, Because she's one of these ones: interferes in everyone's business. She has it in for me.

Natalie touched a hard shoulder straining against his shirt. Tab tensed. She thought about how when she met him at the office (not even in a bar, not even with drink in him) he'd put her hand on his work shirt and said, Feel that. Do you know what type of material that is? No? That's boyfriend material, that is. He loved it that she was as tall as him. He loved that she had Libbie and was settled. Didn't dress *slutty*. Didn't drink.

What business did she interfere in, Tab?

Tab turned to her slightly, still averted his eyes. There was this girl I was seeing, he said. They lived near each other in the estate. One of these girls who likes drama. Likes to tell lies. Wasn't Charmaine's ma there, in court, like victim support? You don't drop the charges when you're in the right, do you? Tab leaned over, lifted a lime wedge and pressed it into the top of his beer. He took a sip. He looked at the knife. I asked you a question, he said. Nat, do you drop the charges when you're in the right?

There must've been some kind of mistake, Natalie said taking her hands from the back pockets of her jeans. She looked into the hall, the party dribbling out of the living room. An arm. A leg. Music. Lights. The upstairs bathroom door was open, spilling its milky stream on to the landing.

OUCH!

Thank you, Stephen, for asking me to be your best man. That means that if anyone asks who the best man is around here, I want you all to remember it's me. Not joking! That means that today, forget Stephen and Mags, I'm the one everyone should be talking about because I'm the best man, okay?

When you are best man you have to do loads of meaningless things: pick up suits, arrange the stag. You have to remember what you are allowed to say and what has to stay out of the speech. Here is the list of things I can say:

[pulls a piece of paper from his inside pocket, one inch squared]

and here is what I am not allowed to talk about:

[pulls a piece of paper from his back trouser pocket, it unravels and reaches the floor. The crowd laugh]

Stephen even had me doing things that had nothing to do with the wedding. For example, did you know that Stephen and Mags are getting some home improvements done at the minute? They left me a key for the house and told me to wait for the carpet fitter. I have to relay a message from the fitter, then we can begin. Stephen, he says that your carpet has arrived but there's a delay with the stuff that goes underneath. I told him today was your wedding day and he said, That's alright then, he'll be getting his underfelt tonight anyway.

[some of the crowd laugh, some groan]

Honestly, you could laugh a little harder, it's difficult, you know, being up here in front of all these strangers. And if you think it's bad for me, just think about Stephen, he doesn't know any of youse.

[Ouch! shouts a member of the bridal party]

Did someone just say, ouch? That *is* funny. Stephen doesn't actually mind that his family aren't here, and how many are there, Stephen? Ten of youse? And think about all those extended families. No, don't feel sorry for Stephen that his family aren't here. He's good aren't you, Stephen? But still... no one... no one at all. Yes, ouch!

[laughter]

When Stephen asked me to be his best man, I didn't have to think twice about it. It was more like three... hundred times. I thought, doesn't he have someone else he knows, someone he doesn't see once a year, like he sees me. Apart from that little spell when we didn't see each other at all. But the less said about that the better. Eh, Steve?

I'm going to start by telling you how I first met Stephen and tell you some stories that will make him redder than the ketchup on your McDonalds there. Honest to God, Stephen, couldn't you have at least paid for a decent meal, all these people coming here, all Mags's family and friends, they deserve something to settle their stomachs after watching you pure eat the face of her for all them pictures. Seriously, Stephen, what are you going to do with them photos? Put them on the wall? Is there any room left? For those of you that don't know, and I'm sure there are a lot of you, this is Stephen's fourth wedding, apart from the time in Maghaberry when Bubba made Stephen his wife, but we'll leave that time aside and just count the husband times. You'd think that by the fourth time you'd know what you're doing and not... sorry, I'm going off script here. But anyway, I think we should raise our glasses to his stamina.

[holds his glass up]

To Stephen.

Right, back to the business in hand. How I met Stephen... How did I meet Stephen? Now there is a story in itself. And I can't even remember it. Stephen Kent is just one of those people who was always about, you know. Just, everywhere.

Hold up. I've lost that page. Let me just... No. I've lost it.

Right, forget that.

Stephen Kent was a friend of a friend and we used to go out to the rugby and the bar. Then, Stephen went a bit off the rails, I'm sure that's alright to say, isn't it? I saw him from time to time. He wasn't always such a pleasure to be round, I'm not sure that he is now. Just joking. No, he's not a bad cretin at all. I think it is testament to his character that he has it in him to reel everything back in and give it a go again.

Fair play, Stephen. I mean that.

When you look at Mags you can see the motivation. Am I right? Doesn't she have a lovely pair of t___

[gasps from the crowd]

Teeth. I was going to say teeth. Lovely pair. Just the two. [looks sheepishly at Mags] Too far? Stop looking at me like that, Stephen. No, really, Mags, you are looking simply stunning and even you Stephen are looking simply... Well, we'll leave it at that.

Stephen is a fella I would bump into at the rugby final every year. He'd be hanging around with young fellas from the university area. I think they called Stephen the *daddy* in the gay community. In fact, he has that kind of personality where he mixes well with youngsters. He is the stepdad to seven kids now altogether, but it's not like being a biological dad, everyone, because you can evidently stop being a stepdad when you feel like it.

[groans]

No. Stephen is a great dad. Mags's kids couldn't want for better.

I promised I wouldn't talk for too long. I feel like I've overstayed my welcome already, a bit like Stephen with the Crown Prosecution Service. Less said about that the better, too.

[deathly silence]

You know, I met someone lately and told them that my old... mate? Yeah. We'll go with mate.

[laughter]

Look at you lot laughing like I'm joking. Seriously, I'm not. Anyway, that person I met told me a story about Stephen that I think I might share with you all, if that's alright.

[Stephen wants to know who it is]

What Stephen? It's your mother. No, really, she said something nice. Stephen's mother told me.

[Stephen tells him to move on]

What? No, seriously, it's fine. It's a nice thing.

[Leave it, Paddy, says Stephen]

Oh dear, I've said something wrong. She just said she loved you, that's all. I'll leave it be…

He's always been a rugby fan, has Stephen. That's how I met him. That's how he met Mags too. She plays hooker. Kidding. No, I believe it was Tinder he met her on, and that's fine. I believe Stephen used to be good at rugby and he had an injury that stopped him. I was sad to hear that. Really, I was.

So you can see he was always sporty, though you wouldn't know it to look at him now. Time and a career sitting on your arse is an absolute cunt, isn't it?

[groans]

No, you *can* say cunt at a wedding. I already checked. It's fine. Now, I want you all to look at that wall, over there. No, over there. Hit the slides, mate.

[a photo is projected]

Here is our Stephen as a young man. I know, bet you wish you'd met him then instead, Mags.

[murmuring in the crowd]

Alright everyone, calm down, he wasn't Brad Pitt exactly. But he wasn't bad either. And look, next image. There he was aged fifteen at school. He's the big one with the face like a Lurgan spade and the bad haircut. Look at all those kids in the school. No, hold on, that's not a school, that's someone's living room. Ten of them. No TV in that house. You can see that, can't you, in a couple of ways.

[another photo is projected]

And here, with his mother and father, when he was a baby. Stephen, I do believe I see a tear. No?

[Stephen shakes his head]

Look at him, no tears here. He's all man, our Stephen. I have a couple more photos, but to be honest I think you already saw them on *Crimewatch*, so… moving on.

Stephen drives a taxi now. It's an honest path, provided it's for a real company. Actually, I feel my phone buzz in my pocket, must have been from when we were told to put them on silent for the service. Let me just get this.

[groans]

Hello, yes? That's me, Paddy, what is it? This is really bad timing, I'm kind of in the middle of something. What am I doing? Seriously, you want to know.

[crowd grow restless]

I'm actually giving the speech at a wedding. Yes, I am the best man, thanks for saying. Who's wedding? It's Stephen Kent and Mags… Kent. Yes, you know him from [whispers] *Crimewatch*. Stephen's tapping his watch here, you'll have to speed it up. Okay, I'll pass on the message, and who will I say it calling. Alright. Bye bye bye bye.

Stephen, that was the 1930s, they say they want their hair gel back.

[laughter]

Honest to god, you are like something from *The Great Gatsby*, you ever heard of it? No? Didn't think so. It's a book. You know, like *Dick & Dora*? It's about a young guy who... You know what, I'll tell you later.

Well Stephen Kent, Jay Gatsby, or what was the alias you were going by when you were milking the court service?

[sharp intake of breath from someone]

Never mind that, can I just say that you are a good guy. You are. Well... you aren't a bad guy. And it's good to see you land on your feet. And you, Mrs Kent the fourth, have landed on your feet too, and now I suggest that you run. And keep your cheque book under lock and key. And passwords and PINs.

Now I want you all to get on your feet and raise your glasses and join me in toasting the happy couple.

[everyone stands]

The happy couple!

[The happy couple! Glasses chink]

PLAYOFFS

With Daddy away for a spot of on-the-road business, Mam tapped on my bedroom door with the notion of going to Bray in her red Ford Cortina. She'd intended to fit in some of the normal reasons anyone from school went there, or so she claimed, but the tone of her voice told me she had prearranged—at least with herself —the detour which would see that we never got there at all. I knew once we were close by she'd announce that we were to call in on my grandparents in Enniskerry and any hopes of enjoying ourselves on the promenade would be dashed, yet how much fun could I have had with my own mother, me, seventeen as I was then?

At my grandparents' cottage it was always the same push and pull, my sloping, slow-footed Granddad begging us to stay, us, fresh ears for his stories. He was always so admiring it made me uncomfortable.

I've had a word with the Gods, Connie. You'll be the first Kidd to university, he would say.

O'Donnell-Kidd, Gran would correct him, rolling her eyes like eggs in marbling.

Mam would remind them that she'd gone to university, and Gran would remind her that, yes, she had, but then she'd got that currant bun in the oven, nodding toward me, her face feigning indifferent reserve.

No, once we got near Bray Mam was at last truthful of her intentions, in part at least.

We'll pop over, briefly only, Mam said. And once Granddad had his hand around her arm, guiding her through the cottage and into the garden to enjoy, How gorgeous it is — you don't get that bloom in Dublin, Minnie.

There was no getting out.

In the gorgeous garden that it truly was — although I didn't appreciate such things back then — Mam sat in the deck chair next to mine, side on, her profile blanched by the clean sun and against the wall Granddad had painted peach, she looked like one of the cameos in Gran's jewellery box. Mam's hair was all fixed up with the odd strand tumbling down the nape of her neck and those shoulder pads puffed up like they had a life of their own.

Stapled to a wooden crisscross trellis were full-headed, red-maned roses that ballooned and burst their petals all over the pavement. Every time I looked there was a new cast-off. I tallied them up. A flutter from the corner of my eye would see I had to start again. Adding up the ones that had landed concave and the ones that fell convex as though they were hiding something underneath, there were less of the latter. The ratio was on average 5:4. The counting helped me look absorbed when Granddad told another recycled story.

Granddad talked about the 18th-century Palladian house that had been damaged in a fire some years ago, he dithered about between fourteen and fifteen years like a dog deciding the best place to kick up the earth and plank his bones. The house remained a carcass.

When is someone going to make the house better? Mam asked looking upset by the notion of it.

I never took Mam for a building person before that, just a people person, or a women's person to be precise, their philosophies and injustices, Mam, changing people's minds and going about it all wrong with the very woman who brought her into the world.

When Granddad spoke it came out of the side of a mouth speckled with short white whiskers that always grazed your cheek when you eventually were allowed to bid him goodbye, *till next time.* He ran his eye over his daughter. I like what you've done with your hair, Minnie.

Oh, Da! Mam cried.

Let your father admire you if he wants to, Gran said.

Can I stop him anyway? Mam widened her eyes like the girls in school did when they were being facetious.

Be glad somebody loves you, Gran told her.

Well, that is the height of ridiculousness! Mam huffed.

The garden went silent for a while after. Flies flicked about. Gran was a good old age then, her hair was pinned up too, I had to do a double take between her and Mam. Mam would have thrown every pin away if she'd have seen what I had.

A cloud drifted across the sky and the sun considered early retirement before slogging on. We had to put our chairs across to the other side of the garden to catch it up. Granddad leant over before making himself comfortable again on his lounger, his fountain pen bursting like a black grape inside a shirt pocket.

Take it off, Gran said, her fingers flapping like wings against her palms as he slowly and ham-fistedly undid each button and handed the shirt to her. She stood examining the blot like a person being psychoanalysed, being asked what the shape of things meant to her. I knew she wasn't seeing bunnies, that was for sure. Dark liquid had pooled in the crease of skin under Granddad's breast. When Gran had returned from steeping the material in the sink, she picked an apple from the tree and after a brief swipe inside her apron handed it to me.

There, that's everything a bit more Protestant looking, she said.

I was waiting on Mam to tell her she should be glad Daddy wasn't there, he didn't like that kind of talk. But Mam gave her head a shake instead and slumped down her chair, she tilted her face at the sun, a strange gleam of contentment about her. She stayed like that for about a half hour then coughed for my attention and nodded toward the door.

We'll have to head off, Mam broadcast.

No you don't, it's not often you call these days, Granddad said, his brown hands on the shock of white belly.

Minnie only calls when Dermot's not home and she wants her dinner made, Gran said.

Mam shot her a look. The hard green apple with the brown star dotted around its stalk held my concentration. I began counting each speck on its skin.

Ah now, Judy! Granddad said to Gran, then me, Tell her, Connie, tell your ma to stay for dinner.

It doesn't seem as if we're wanted, Mam said.

The fruit looked *too* unripe, but I, for some reason, always became a different person in the village. So did Mam. I ate things I shouldn't have and Mam said things she always regretted. I stuck my teeth into the skin and took a bite, moving it around my mouth, my throat already telling me it was letting nothing down.

Where's Dermot working this week? Granddad asked.

Up North, Mam answered.

Give your father a civil answer, Gran said.

Did I not?

You're as odd as two left bloody feet, Minnie.

Dermot's in Newry. Is that alright, Mother?

If an answer came from Gran it came so slow it got lost somewhere in the vacuum between them. Gran went inside, looking increasingly shrunken, and was gone for hours cooking dinner inside while we cooked ourselves outside. When we got it, dinner took so very little time to finish off, it hardly seemed worth all the effort. Granddad insisted we all sit on, go outside again till the summer's day turned into a summer's night, and in that time Mam found reason to flit in and out of the house.

When we managed to pull away from the home and Granddad's rotating tales of the village that were told with his thumb hooked to our wrists — and his eyes on some indiscriminate spot behind our heads that made Daddy call him *the stargazer* — Mam backed the car over the gravel and away from the cottage altogether, adjusting and readjusting her mirror.

She drove just out of sight of the house, pulled the car over and the keys from the ignition. Mam threw them at me, clasped half inside hands I had instinctively drawn to my chest.

Drive, Connie. I've had five whiskeys, she said. She did look rough. Mam's chignon, as she called it, was crestfallen.

I haven't even done my test yet, I told her.

I'll keep you right. You know how to get to Bray from here and Dublin from Bray... surely to god.

It's the roundabouts, I said.

Waken me when we get to them. I'll keep you riiiiight, she said impatiently, deflating with a sigh that spilt the stench of her secret nips into the warm air inside the vehicle. Gawd, she's an auld bitch.

Who? I asked, as if I didn't know.

Who'd'ya think? Me ma. That, Connie, is the very reason your father and I only had you and no others. Their family was overstretched already. She resented me, ya know! The youngest. Her little accidental.

I rolled my eyes heavenward and put my full beam on, it bounced over the darkening corduroy fields as we turned our backs on the mountains.

Do you want some ketchup for the chip on your shoulder? I asked her.

What in the world did you just say? Her expression rumbled and when it broke she cracked full with laughter. Ketchup for the chip on yer shoulder? Where'd'ya hear that one?

Mam laughed the whole way up the road till she fell asleep. Every time I had to nudge her awake for road directions or reminders of the rules, she would remember it as an afterthought and tee-hee *ketchup* to herself.

*

True to his word Granddad made the stars somehow align: Trinity College accepted Constance O'Donnell-Kidd as one of their own. I was a raw recruit only underdone by Sidney Sittlington. Good old smiley Sidney from The Student's Union, the boy who would carry my books and ask me if I wanted to accompany him to this reading and that dance. I knew it was because I was local and he didn't have a clue where he was going. Truth be told he liked to be led, but then didn't we all!

At times I wondered why I'd settled so easily when there were better blokes around. Yet Sidney had a knack of opening my ears. He used phrases from the west that I'd never heard. I loved to hear what was going to come out of his mouth next.

Sidney made me Mrs Sittlington. Before he did I went to tell Gran in person.

She'd laughed. Where will that monstrosity go into your own name? Sittlington-O'Donnell-Kidd? She went on to try out every variation. You'd be better off with a number. He would too, bloody Sidney Sittlington!

It was the first time she had used that edge of her tongue with me. I have to admit there was a transmogrification after that, she didn't seem like the little old lady with the wicked sense of humour. I blew it out of proportion in my mind and later realised if anything she was just dreadfully unhappy, even though she had Granddad who was a better husband altogether than Daddy was to Mam or Sidney to me. Oh dear — as if other people were what made folk happy.

After her remarks I'd pushed my dessert bowl away and said, Those apples you put in your crumble are always horribly bitter, Gran.

If Mam had been there she'd have lapped it up, she still had a pleasant stretch in her stomach at the taste of the line second-hand.

*

The first time I brought Sidney to meet my parents, Daddy had taken to him like a fly to sticky paper. Daddy loved that he was going to spend his life in halls and theatres instead of roads and other people's living rooms, selling kids the principles of others. Stuff that took up no space in the van: nice, compact little way of earning.

You can be your own boss... and Sidney, they're buying you. I think that's fan-bloody-tastic! Daddy said.

Steady on, I laughed.

No, Connie, people will always need educating.

Daddy didn't know that Sidney had less knowledge than he liked to admit. Even I didn't know that he had a strange sense of himself that made parting with his insignificant knowledge difficult, even though it wasn't hard for the kids to find out things without him, that's what libraries were for. He was going to be the one to get the message from pillar to post. At that point in our relationship Sidney had a different sense of himself that I still much prefer, he seemed to believe that he would make a good teacher. I longed to see how he would do it.

Mam came in from a meal out with friends and met me with a slow smile. She couldn't conceal her surprise that Sidney was as he was.

Well hullo, Sidney, she slurred, slopping coffee into a mug and leaning back against the kitchen counter to get a better look at us both together, as if she was taking a mental photograph. Mam took Sidney by the sleeve into the lounge where the fire crackled in the hearth like glass beads falling on tiles.

Sit down, sit down, Mam said. Tell me all about Galway.

Sidney eased into the fabric sofa. As he spoke his face grew more staid, almost as though he had practised some speech that Daddy hadn't required because he's been delighted simply by the university link and sensibly cropped hair. Everything Sidney said was met by an exaggerated nod or shake of the head as Mam overegged it.

I filled the kettle again and make a pot for the whole lot of us, though Sidney had been encouraged only too easily to join her with a nightcap, he obviously thought it would kill every bird over the River Liffey with one smooth skimming amber pebble.

Mam unearthed the after-dinner mints from the cabinet, I let one melt on my tongue. Sidney refused any. Do you want to go? I asked in a whisper, surely he was sick of Daddy gushing and Mam with her insider jokes, giggling at the entirety of what anybody had to say.

Not at all. Sure this is great, he said taking everything in, and I didn't know who to be the more mortified of.

When it got too late to keep my eyes open a second longer, and I had heard more about Sidney's background from what he told Mam than I'd gleaned in a whole year, I knew it was time.

Sidney, you have class tomorrow, I said.

So do you, Connie! Mam said. She watched Sidney to make sure that he wasn't the type to quash my dreams.

Yes, so do I.

Lovely meeting you, Mrs... *O'Donnell-Kidd*? He paused.

Kidd, dear. Minnie Kidd, Mam said in a James Bond kind of way that made a *Jesus H Christ* rip from my throat.

What's wrong with Connie? she asked. If you ask me, Sidney... you could do so much better for yourself.

I practically pulled him out of the door, there was a soft swish of it closing along the carpet. We sat in silence on the way back to our little flat I'd made him promise not to let slip about.

Do you want to talk about anything? he asked.

So you're in the mood for talking to me now, I said, knowing I was being fairly ridiculous.

*

Way back in our early courtship, as my Granddad would have said, Sidney and I made an arrangement, he drew dibs on calling our second child a name of his choosing. We never considered we would get two at once, two girls, eight minutes apart. I called the first baby Phoebe, the one who was born without a cry, then handed over to Sidney the responsibility of naming the next. He took no joy in it. It grated on me how he used to be excited by the prospect, far more than I even, yet he just let a pretty-samey type two syllabic noise slip out, no particular thought put into it.

Sophie then, he said

Why? I asked.

They go nice, like anagrams of each other, Sidney said. It was always words with Sidney, till it wasn't. I wanted my children to be individuals, to have names that were mountain and math. That was part of the appeal of a name each, hidden till the children revealed themselves, or an obstetrician did the job for them, too laid back for such drama were my two daughters, in no hurry to get anywhere.

I wanted them to be poles apart but they pasted themselves together as they grew like a road that seemed to have been put there by nature, but hadn't, but had been moulded by the feet before, over generations and over centuries.

Sidney spoke of having more children. He was a good one for that, for talking about having children and forgetting about the rearing of them. I'd learnt my lesson from wrestling two children into all-in-ones and double buggies, holding one child in my arms and balancing a bottle on a pillow for the other, worrying myself demented that the pillow would slip or that I, dog-tired, would succumb to my sleep and a baby would choke to death.

I dressed both of them in blue and gave Phoebe and Sophie footballs to play with. They gravitated toward dollies and pink. Smooth and frilled. Happiness and harmony. And despite my refusal to dress them the same, they wouldn't be made individual. They were two halves of the same person, even slept puzzle-pieced together, it didn't matter that they weren't inside me anymore. They shared every choice.

The girls—yes I know! I eventually yielded and grouped them together myself, categorised by their birth number and gender— as they got bigger were easily occupied by one another. Friends complained that their children needed to be constantly occupied and could not entertain themselves, I was proud of Phoebe and Sophie's bond. They were independent fast, of me at least.

Time passed without juncture. Sidney gave up the baby argument and settled on disputing the small stuff, not one for larger playoffs he couldn't win. We moved to Galway were the girls grew wildly and when they were five I began to sense that Sidney's family felt imposed on by our need of their help with childcare. When things should have been getting easier they proved me wrong. We moved back to Dublin where it was decided that I would stop surveying and remain at home.

Daddy had had a liver transplant in the months before the first Christmas we all spent together. I was glad to see him out of hospital and looking well.

I can't believe it's been a year since I held these two beauties, he said scooping Phoebe and Sophie into his arms.

They really go from being babies to little girls at this age, Mam said, looking somewhat softer all round, grannyish even, she was standing in the doorway of her study where she hugged Sidney and told him of a book she bought for him. It wasn't part of his Christmas present, just a little something extra. She walked inside, I followed, there were her old books I used to read snippets off when I was young, Mam's écriture feminine, they had powdered in a room that was starting to have the musty smell of age—like a school or a church. I didn't see which book Sidney took from her and slipped into his long winter coat. When I recalled about it later that night, just before I nodded off, he told me he already had it but hadn't wanted to hurt her feelings. Still, it was a good one.

Connie, check the tatties, I've got goose fat all raring to go, Mam said.

When I looked around I saw her, parcels in hand, on her knees with the children. Daddy winked at me. Been looking after me the best, your mam, he said.

At the table Sidney was asked to carve the bird. The girls snapped crackers. The whole scenario felt like something from a feel-good American movie, the perfect ending if you will. Even Daddy ridding his mouth of all the turkey's spittable bits and refilling it with cava seemed endearing.

Dermot, should you be? Mam asked him, she had pure orange in her glass, the little segment bits were highlighted by the candles that were burning down, the flames dancing like moths.

I'm here for a good time, not a long time, Daddy told her.

The donor's family would love to hear that! Mam told him all in good jest. She raised her glass, looked over the girls, her eyes filmy with tears. Girls, you've been so well behaved. I just want to make a toast: to the Sittlingtons coming back to Dublin! You're the most divine children I've ever seen and I love you very much. She got up from her chair to go and cup each one around their giggling faces and kiss their cheeks.

Nanaaaa, Phoebe cried laughing.

It was the first time I had heard the word *love* come out of Mam's mouth. It seemed to have been hardwired out of her vocabulary. I felt my own eyes glaze too, nothing that a good sniff wouldn't shake.

So you found the secret to well-behaved children, Daddy said pausing, waiting for my absent response. Is it like hamsters? Better in pairs? They say they're nasty little buggers on their own.

Company, Sidney said, succinctness becoming his forte.

*

As the children became teenagers I realised that despite their long limbs and toothy grins they would surpass any awkward stage. Where their beauty came from was a mystery, when I was outwardly average and Sidney not even that. Besides they were more than just their looks. It would have been a nice problem to have, yet it worried me they would find it harder to be taken seriously. Even though I knew neither had the inclination to become some sort of airhead model, I never gave them an inkling how gorgeous they were, and they really were, and still are, equal gorgeous girlness.

Just when I thought I had Sophie and Phoebe pinned, they went and surprised me with different university courses on their applications, and they seemed to surprise each other too. That was the cherry on the bakewell. They scrawled their first choices on a page each, course title beneath, location beneath that. I counted to three and they turned their pages around at the same time. Phoebe had put down Business with Economics while Sophie wanted to study Women's Studies.

Do you think I'm being silly? Sophie asked.

I looked up, her eyes were on me.

Me? Why would *I*? I asked.

Well, you look surprised, she said.

I couldn't picture them out of Ireland, one in Scotland, the other in Manchester. The idea had feet and would soon start running. It was all a jolt.

I don't think you're silly at all. Maybe naive, I admitted.

I knew that. You having us and all...

I'm named after Constance Markievicz you know, the great Irish socialist icon. Sure your Nana's a feminist. So am I.

Phoebe loitered storkily, tucking her hair behind a shell-like ear, looking from me to her sister and back again. But the conversation had slid off.

A month later Grainne, an old friend of mine, was throwing a party for her elder son Lucas's wedding. The girls, Sidney and I ended up in four separate corners of the hotel's function room. Phoebe danced with the little children up well past their bedtimes, her hair swept over her face like a tide. Sophie, our designated driver, schmoozed with the senior relatives laughing away, always with spirit to spare. I felt a tap on my shoulder. It was Grainne herself.

Beautiful reception, I said over the music.

Your girls are the type I'd have hated in school. I thought I'd misheard her at first. Just through jealousy... is what I'm saying.

Oh, Grainne! Me too, I thought.

You must be proud, she shouted, I watched her lips.

I smiled and nodded, then leaned in close again. And you of Lucas. And of Michael too, I repaid her.

Oh yes, Michael is getting back on his feet, a little one to look after now by himself. Grainne nodded at Michael, his hand holding Sophie's hair gently away from her ear as he spoke into it. She was looking ahead, in a daze, blinking and smiling. The kids have found their own way, Grainne said. They know what they found themselves and what they heard when we spoke. Do you agree, Connie?

I think that's what she said, I was watching Sophie then watching Sidney. He was still sat at the table, still immersed in talk like I only ever saw him in the company of other men, in that impenetrable bubble I left him to, punctuating every important statement with a stab of his finger in the air. When his company had disbanded, Sidney grappled with his chair till he stood at the side of the dance-floor like a wooden pawn ready to slide across to me and pull me away from Grainne's side into a dance. I waved over to the girls. Home time!

Outside we ran, half-dragging Sidney to the car with our coats over our heads. He'd won the no-need-for-an-umbrella argument, now he was too stocious to feel the upshot of winning.

Mum, I've been thinking the past few weeks and I know now that you can be a mother and be a feminist too, Sophie told me, her face darkly glistening, the reflection of the pouring weather on her skin as she purred the engine up.

I looked over my shoulder. In the backseat Phoebe had parked her head in the crook of her father's neck, they fell asleep before we were out of the car park. I leant over Sophie's arm and put the window wipers on full pelt wanting to put my hands in the loamy air between us instead, pull all the distance away, pull the handbrake up, stop in that rare moment that we were all in the same space that only would get rarer.

Sophie was tired and giddy, if I didn't know better I'd have thought a bit tipsy.

What's so funny? Soph, I asked her.

You really want to hear this? She dipped her eyes at me.

Go on then.

Mum, do you know what I want to be? Sophie wet her lips with her tongue to ease the words out. A mother. More than anything.

Electrical synapses took charge through me and I couldn't explain it. It wasn't disappointment, she would make a fantastic parent. How could she get it wrong? Sophie — like her sister — had the best of every member in the family. The whole flawless package. I tried to say that but it stuck somewhere.

I'll tell you something no one else will: motherhood is the loneliest job on the planet, I said this instead and I don't know why. I wanted to pinch my skin. I closed my eyes and listened to the tyres sloshing on the road, heard her breathing outplay the rain, not bearing to look as a cry carved from her throat.

That's not to say that you and Phoebe aren't the best things in my life. By far, I added, perhaps too late, but Sophie had taken a hand from the wheel and put it on mine. I didn't want her to end up like us. Too many women lose custody of their own ambition.

Mum, you don't have to say... She wasn't crying but chuckling to herself.

When I looked into Sophie's eyes again I saw there was no upset, just wide open spaces where pity couldn't hide.

ALIVE AND TWITCHING

It wasn't as if she trafficked in sentimentality—Maralin didn't. She allowed herself one jacket. A keepsake. If such a term could be given to the chalky grey coat of Alfred's. One year on it still hung by the kitchen door. It had lost his scent months ago, and now smelled like the room. Basil, sage and thyme.

Cherith bleeped her car locked and sped up to walk alongside. How's Maralin this morning? Cherith asked, in the habit of addressing people as if asking after a mutual friend.

Fine, Maralin said, marching toward the hospital.

Do anything nice last night?

Ah not much. Maralin swiped for them both, keyed in her passcode. The night before may have been a Saturday but all days lumped into one. Nothing special about any of them. Even Alfred's anniversary, the day itself, needn't be anything singular.

Did you… do anything nice? she asked, returning the pretence of interest.

A movie with a takeaway, Cherith said.

As often as she had heard people say the same thing, Maralin wondered how the two went together. Movies were surely something sweet to enjoy with popcorn. Chocolate even. What did she know anymore? People watched horrid films as if real life wasn't bitter enough. If Maralin had a cup of soup in her hand and a soap opera on the TV that was that—her version. She would hardly boast about it.

Maralin and Cherith left their top layers in the store and headed through to the office where the night receptionists slouched over the desks.

I was glad of a movie, you know, Cherith whispered shoving her handbag under the desk, the night woman's knees pointing the other direction to accommodate. My Paddy blathers on and I'm too punctured. I want to say, listen, I talk all day, I can't be annoyed tonight.

Why don't you? Maralin asked.

Ruth stood to let her sit in the swivel seat. Maralin pumped the chair to the perfect height and put the back upright. Ruth and the other woman—who Maralin had never bothered to find out the name of—logged off their telesets and unplugged their earphones. For a while, a few years ago, when Maralin had been more involved, she learnt about her past colleagues and their families. Now she barely acknowledged the people in the room as she fitted her headset over her hair and piped herself into the system. She swivelled around so that she was facing the white wall with the hospital trust calendar tacked to it, and thought, *here goes nothing.*

It never ceased to amaze Maralin how well she had the patter down. It was unthought, even replayed when she was in bed at night, when only the owls hooting in the trees outside her cottage could break the running commentary in her head. Some nights were worse than others.

Hello, GP out of hours. This call will be recorded. What is the emergency? Cherith said behind her, a few hours into a busy morning. She was sticking to the script which meant that Brian was slicing through the space between them. He stopped and stood over Cherith, listening to her call and giving the thumbs up.

Make yourself unavailable after, he said. He reached for a sheet of paper from the edge of the desk.

Clearly distracted Cherith squinted. Bless you, Rebecca. Just come on down and the Doctor will see you, love. Take care now, Miss Stoops. She pressed the red button and looked up at Brian.

Okay, we have the stats here. He ran his appraising eye over her and his finger over the figures.

Cherith smoothed her skirt under her, leaving her hands wedged defensively between her seat and her legs.

You have to make sure that you're saying what is the emergency?

I did. She gestured at the phone.

Every time? A muscle jumped in his jaw.

Brian, who wrote this script? It's very antagonistic, Cherith said in a conspiratorial voice.

Maralin ducked her head so as not to be included. Too late, Brian nodded to indicate she wouldn't be forgotten. He followed back along his initial evaluation, You're meant to make the callers think—do I really need medical attention? We don't want to put Jason under more pressure. And remember to say that the doc will call them back. Don't invite patients down here to clog the waiting room up.

People don't like that line about the emergency, Cherith resumed. A frown gathered on her.

You have to say it. And Cherith, you're still taking too long, whereas Maralin doesn't spend enough time. He wavered a finger between them like a barometer's needle. You could both learn from each other.

Don't we even out then? Cherith asked.

Doesn't work like that.

Maralin heard her phone click and a new call come through. Hello, GP out of hours. This call will be recorded. What is the emergency?

Brian nodded. Maralin felt his eyes, she turned away, entered the name and date of birth the woman on the other end had given her, and she lowered her voice. The twelfth of April?

Yes.

Cain Kirkcaldy?

Yes.

He's not on the system, Maralin said.

Is he not? the woman asked before proceeding to go into detail about cramps and contents of bowels and bellies, or rather the lack thereof. Maralin stopped her short to curtly remark that the child was not on the system. The woman demanded to know what she meant.

He doesn't exist, Maralin said. She saw the label on her headset wire, it really had no reason to be there. She lifted a pair of scissors and snipped enough off so that she could peel the rest and rub away the gumminess beneath.

Are you fucking kidding me? the woman's voice broke.

You curse one more time and I can hang up on you, Maralin stated with a modicum of delight. She rolled the glue into a ball and flicked it off her finger into the wire bin.

I don't understand what you're on about, Cain's mother paused for Maralin to speak, but she remained quiet, like Alfred used to when he was bargaining a loftily priced purchase. Maralin knew that most people hated silence, they wrongly thought it always had to be filled. Not her. Long sentences enervated her. In person she used unspoken gestures to get by, on the phone she could only be still.

He's registered with a doctor. He has a medical card. Do you need the number? Mrs Kirkcaldy asked, at least Maralin assumed she was a Mrs Kirkcaldy, though she daren't say it. Few mothers shared their children's surnames anymore. Brian had told her to side-step that route altogether.

You've never used the out of hours for Cain. He doesn't exist on our system.

You said that. Maralin could hear teeth gritting down the line. Does that mean he never can be?

No, I'll put Cain's details up... there, he's on it now.

The woman returned Maralin's serve, Was all that fuss really necessary?

Excuse me?

Can you get the doctor to call me back? I have a sick child here.

And what's your emergency?

I don't think it's an emergency or I'd take him to the emergency room, wouldn't I? If it wasn't Sunday we'd be at our usual doctor's.

Maralin shook each word out like a red rag. What did you say the emergency is?

Fuck this. I'm coming down there, the woman snapped.

Well then, that is that, Maralin told the dead line.

Brian cast a shadow over her screen, he put his hand on the back of her seat. Unavailable, he instructed. She turned to see him sit beside her. Maralin kept her earphones on for something of a barrier.

You need to lengthen your calls, M, he said.

Since Alfred died Brian reduced her to a letter. Since he had been to the funeral, and the wake, he somehow thought it was grand to do that. She may have been the longest serving *team member* as Brian called the — a relative longevity possibly due to her ability to take abuse without injury, added to her love of pot-stirring — yet really he knew less about Maralin than anyone else who womaned the phones. Maralin didn't know if it was because she was alone and Brian was trying to fill some void — she could've been his mother. Had she had children, they could have been Brian-types, she perished the thought. He had no real interest, but still, he had stopped scheduling her for night shifts after Alfred passed, and had even given her cupcakes in a decorative box on her recent birthday. There were worse things. She knew that.

Don't be afraid of putting your personality in there more. We aren't 999, we can give the patients a bit of our time, M...but good job, all in all.

His words were too faint to take comfort from. Not that she would take comfort from work, being kept busy, maybe, the not giving her mind the chance to wander, definitely.

Brian sent Cherith on her lunch break before he left too.

Maralin pressed the green button and waited for the click. She introduced the call. A man was on the other end, his voice was old, his dialect salty. My insulin's done, he announced. I don't know how I did it but I've run out of meds and I'm going away tonight. Venice.

It was her cue. If she was being told to lengthen her calls then that's what she would do.

Venice, how lovely.

Not really. I'm going to say goodbye to someone. Again, the man said.

Sorry to hear that. She couldn't say right for saying wrong.

I'm going to scatter Beth's ashes. She's a long time gone. Did you know Beth? You're the receptionist from the clinic, I believe.

Just out of hours. I'm in the hospital. Maralin wrapped the cord of the headset around her fingers. I'm locked away in a little safe room.

He laughed. What're they punishing you for?

She told him she never saw the light of day, and he told Maralin she needed to rectify that, and that it was a nice day out. Dry anyway. His tone made her feel momentarily accompanied.

Maralin asked about the weather in Venice. He hadn't checked. He advised her to go sometime, but not for long. Everything could be seen in a weekend, the man told her. He was going to scatter Beth's ashes from one of those gondola things, that's how he worded it. Venice isn't the sweetest smelling of places, the man said.

I've heard, Maralin replied. Though Alfred and I would've just holidayed here.

We've some beautiful beaches, granted. I'm more a stay-at-home man but Beth loved travel, and different languages. I prefer to know what people are saying to me. I do enjoy the food though, their pesto isn't like the jar-muck we get here.

Maralin took her pen and began doodling on her notepad, she spoke almost in a dream, I used to make my own. She had forgotten. He asked her how and she told him. Maralin thought about the basil and all the other herbs lining up on her kitchen windowsill. The last time she made pesto Alfred had said it was too strong. His mouth was burning enough with the chemo, then he stopped eating altogether, and so did she.

You've been kind…listening.

Not at all, Maralin said. It felt like a rehearsal.

She wondered if she had it in her to give as much to every caller. She wondered if she would have a job to go to if she did. It had been forty-five minutes and counting. The man was still talking, telling her about Beth buying a mask in a quaint little shop before, one could decorate their own. It wasn't his type of thing. He might visit the shop again, but was there any point without her?

Don't say goodbye to Beth until you've done all the things you want to, Maralin paused, wondering if she'd taken it a step too far. This is the reason I keep my trap shut, she thought.

Eventually he spoke. Thank God you can't see me, it makes it easier to talk.

It does, she agreed, although she'd always thought the reverse. She never argued half as much out of the office as she did inside. The earphones seemed to trip-wire her brain to handle everything as brusquely as possible. On the monitor a woman was at the door with a crying, flopping child in her arms. Maralin reached over and buzzed her in.

Sylvia Kirkcaldy booted the door closed behind her and shouted along the corridor. Think they can speak to you whatever way they like!

It's been lovely to talk, Mr Grier. Maralin put a note on the man's records for the doctor.

You'll be having to get on, he said.

Sorry, I've a call waiting.

In reality thirty-odd were in a digital join-the-dots line she was at pains to envisage.

Cherith returned. Someone's kicking off, she muttered, don't envy the doc when she gets a hold.

I'm off to lunch. Maralin grabbed her handbag.

At the beach Maralin sat watching as the bay stretched out, tags on dogs jingled against the quiet. She took her sandwich out from the cellophane which she balled up and pressed deep into her coat pocket. Plain ham. She had it every day and was sick to the back teeth of those two white layers, that pink sliver tongue of meat. Hunger had vanished from her so she picked at the bread. An oil tanker on the water gave chuffs that were damply audible. The power station was only just visible on the other side of the water. All detail had been bleached out. Sand gathered inside her shoe and around the toe-seam of her nude pop socks. She slid it off, shook it out, lingered on until the dirty white sky looked as though it had crumbled into a sea of glitter ice.

She tried to picture Alfred gathering up the grains of himself, the grains she'd scattered there. And him strolling out. Out and along the sand. Her perception couldn't deceive her this time, or indeed anytime, but somehow that didn't seem like the good news it really should. Maralin headed back to her car, making her way over brittle twigs and seaweed that crunched underfoot. Her fingers, cold as dulse and purple as a newborn's, rooted for her keys.

Back at work Maralin took her place to begin her spiel.

If it was an emergency I wouldn't phone you. If it was an emergency he'd be dead by now, came a voice. You make me feel sick.

The truth does that to people, Maralin replied, her finger pressed on silent.

At times blind anger consumed her within those white walls. When people spoke of migraines and pains below their ribs, she knew they were in the wrong place for something sinister. Trapped wind most probably.

Cherith's seat squeaked as she pivoted. Is he prone to tonsillitis? Poor wee critter, nothing worse. Cherith held up a page she had scrawled — where did you go? — on to.

Maralin smiled at her and shrugged. Nothing could be said over their calls.

Can I remind you that this call is recorded? Maralin said. Out of hours staff do not get paid to tolerate abuse.

Cherith gave her a commiserative look for every nuisance caller she received.

Neglect is abuse too. Not answering this phone line is neglect, the caller said.

That call slid on to the next until finally it was her last. Maralin let it drag out as pleasantly as she could until the night staff reappeared and she and Cherith could walk back to the car park.

I'm going to Demi-Rose's for my dinner, Cherith said, as if Demi-Rose was someone Maralin should have heard of, and Maralin was certain she'd never heard tell of any Demi-Rose. But she said, Lovely! anyhow, to side-step being brought up to speed.

By the time she reached the cottage the day had lost all its light. Through the kitchen window came the dark smell and the outline, the row of perennial herbs, sitting on the sill waiting to be of use once more and not merely watered and left, watered and left. Maralin pushed the door open. It was stiff and only shifted with a bang from her hip, that stilled her long enough to contemplate leaving it ajar, but once inside, closed all too easily behind.

THE FLOODGATE EFFECT

It was the cool end of August. Wind howled around the old gate lodge like a dog with a trapped tail. I'd stood outside Tanya's bakery twice that month: saw her spin flimsy cake boxes from cardboard sheets, watched her dispel an icing sugar frost from the Perspex counter. At one stage I even went inside. Tanya had been out the back. The thin walls told me she'd not recovered as well I'd often hoped she had. Her daughter served me, all grown up now from when I'd known Carla as a somewhat theatrical girl of six or so. Carla called me out for asking for a cake when I meant to say bun, hence I had to explain they were named differently on the mainland. She might use that information soon, she told me, because she had just won a scholarship to a drama-college in London. But she did not recognise me. When I asked after Tanya, Carla took me for a friend, telling me all about Brandon, like I should have already known.

But I didn't speak to Tanya about it until the night she arrived here. Tanya had halted in the lounge while I beckoned her into my old office. She was taking in the sight of the gas heater, which had remained floored since my I lost my temper at it, and since, seeing as how my mother hadn't changed a thing — not the curtains draped to the floor and blackened in the middle, nor the long-faded floral wallpaper that was clouded in an angled veil thrown onto the ceiling — I knew instinctively what Tanya was looking at.

In the office was my chaise longue, a coffee table and a leather armchair. I let myself fall helplessly into the armchair. Tanya pulled at the cuffs of her fleece. She looked at the box full of ornaments ready for rehousing. I coughed then gestured for her to sit on the chaise.

I'm here for Brandon, was the thing she said.

I know, I told her.

You know? What do you know?

I knew that the boy was in trouble, but how to put it? That was my trouble. Tanya took my silence for more than it was worth. She said, This town never bloody changes. Gossipers and begrudgers. You know they weren't happy for you, for your success. That's the people of this town, Graham. She ran her hand over the back of the chaise, said, Shall I lie down here for old time's sake? Then she sat instead and went quiet as sleep.

I asked her what Brandon was doing with himself and Tanya explained that he was in a bad way.

He's full of spite. The day you left... in the hospital...

I stopped her there, felt it only proper to address it first by apologising.

She looked the room over, sighed and let her eyes finally arrive in my direction. No, Tanya said. I wouldn't have stayed for a guinea pig either.

A guinea pig? I repeated her phrase. It sounded worse on me, like maybe that was exactly what she'd been. Maybe it wasn't a bad choice of words. Though looking at her I knew it wasn't the truth.

Was I more than that? Tanya asked, her face doubtful.

I was in the bakery, I said, you were out the back. I saw Carla.

Tanya allowed herself a smile. Do you remember wee Carla performing? She pointed at the door, to the lounge. Just out there, she said.

My mother thought she was great.

Tanya said, I'm sorry to hear about your mother. She was always so beautiful, her long silver hair. Not grey. Silver. Immaculate. Your family weren't falling apart at the seams. Not like mine.

It's funny how when people say things like that it throws you back, reminds you that things were one way before they were the other. That for some they never seem to change. For me it seemed the world wouldn't stop spinning, not until I got back to mother's house. Even then, with all those little reminders, I didn't go backwards, not to a childhood, not to memories of Tanya recounting her childhood, but to one specific day, one specific night, like everything began and ended then. Memories aren't it. All we have is up to a moment. All that remained of the accident, to me, was a heater, and curtains, and a scent that settled back inside my head and ruffled its feathers.

I remembered that Tanya had a good relationship with her mother and thought I'd return the sentiment, although over the years, the patients, the caseloads, there had been a lot of mothers, and remember how there was a sharp U-turn away from blaming the mother? It is no longer fashionable. Out with refrigerator mothers. In with taking responsibility for oneself. And what of the refrigerator sons? I am one, granted, but self-diagnosis is no recommendation.

Tanya said that her mother was dead too. Alzheimer's. Gone the scenic route: is that what you'd say... in the business? she asked. You've a name for everything after all. Tanya allowed herself to tear up. I remembered then that she was always a pretty crier. Easily recovered.

Tanya, I know it's none of my business anymore, I said, but did you ever find out if she knew?

No. That left quite a gap in your book, didn't it? she asked.

I asked her if she was cross about the book.

Cross? Me? No! Didn't I tell you I'd always dreamt of being thinly veiled?

I shuffled uncomfortably. Tanya seemed to enjoy seeing this. No one knows it was me... I hope, she said. Well, I do but. Anyway... Tanya stood abruptly, sprang forward and lifted a cake-stand from the ornament box, held it up to the window. I was going to offer it to her when she said, Did your mother bake, Graham?

I told her I couldn't remember Mother baking anything much. Maybe arranging cakes — there I went with the cakes again! buns even — onto her cake-stands for tea afternoons with the bridge ladies.

Mine did, said Tanya, baked batches of them, then I would lock myself up in the bathroom and gorge. And you know what usually happened after that.

I thought you were better, Tanya. I hoped you were.

Is it visible on me? She set the stand down, delicately, her little finger stayed aloft, knuckles grazed, hands red-raw. I didn't tell Tanya about the sounds that came through the bakery wall, the flush, the embarrassment on Carla whose volume peaked to disguise it. After I left the bakery I got a newspaper from Joe Hamill's next door and, when I passed Sweet Sensations, Tanya was at the sink, washing her hands incessantly.

It's a shame, I said. You seemed to be doing much better.

She looked really angry with me now. For God's sake, Graham! You thought you'd cured me, with your words, your... hocus-pocus. My child's face was ruined! Two black lines from that heater you still have lying out there *on its back*. There was a lilt at the end of her sentence, it carried her words up like an accusation.

Another relic that has failed to leave this place, she said. Everything bad fucking sticks. Everything I care about gets up and walks. But you? You left me without the one person I could talk to, Graham. You. She inhaled, straightened up, placed her splayed hands on her knees, composed. What do you call this? she asked.

Call what? I looked around to find a clue written somewhere.

What happens to me in this room? What do you call what happens to me when I'm with you? I can never stop it.

I shouldn't have left so soon after what happened to Brandon, I admitted. It burdened me for some time, the way things do until there are new things to take over the job.

But you're back now, said Tanya. Back to head the local University. I couldn't believe that when I read it.

Maybe. There's been a change of plan.

But it said in the paper, *Local Mental Health Pioneer back to take up important post*. But still...you're leaving again regardless.

It was never going to be permanent. Just a whim. Just timing... like everything else. Mother had just died, a colleague recommended me. I didn't think it through.

This room, geez! I still feel the same when I am inside these walls.

I don't know if that is a good thing or a bad thing, I said.

But I am glad to see you again. My Brandon is like you, he has great insight into people's minds. It's the scars. It makes you know things when you have to live with scars. They got worse over the years, operations and skin, it stretches. The injury was far worse than we could have realised.

I feel awful. I never...

Didn't your mother update you?

We never mentioned the fire outright. No, that sounded heartless. I hadn't visited her in years, if truth be told. After I took the Birmingham job it was phone calls. Letters.

Tanya nodded, she picked something from the cuff of her fleece, a hair maybe. Let it float to the floor. I saw your mother a few times in my bakery, Tanya said. She would ask after Brandon. Always seemed to linger as if she wanted to say something more.

It seems like yesterday he and Carla were playing about.

Does it? It feels like a million years have gone by to me.

I read in the local papers Mother sent that Brandon went away for treatment. I was always curious to know.

We are only limited by our curiosity, Graham, said Tanya. And my number has never changed. She rubbed the couch arm with her thumb. In your first book, she said, well, it's been a while since I read it, but you said that when I was lying here on your sofa... telling you all about my family, about the children's father... Archie, she added in case I had forgotten his name. And I had. Graham, you said it was leather, this couch, but I'm pretty certain it's leatherette.

It would have seemed wrong for me to smile, but I did want to. Can you see why I never got in touch? I said. I didn't want to seem as though I was... *researching* Brandon.

Do you remember the lines were like smudges from a pencil and the tip of Brandon's nose... like it had been dusted with soot? It didn't look too bad at all. But even as I was running to him... I remember feeling like I was trying to run through jelly. I just knew it had to be bad. But I was relieved, you know, when I turned him round to face me. That smell... we could smell it from in here. Who knew disaster had a smell?

Tanya, I said, Mother threw me from the loop. You might say, as she did, that I ran away.

Tanya fixed me in her gaze then, there was something very different in her eyes. She said, Brandon thinks the same thing.

He'd showed at the door a couple of days before, holding my first book in his hand, his hood up, the light stitching itself into the grooves of his scars. The tip of his nose gone like the edge of an island eroded by the elements.

My ma says will you sign this for her? Brandon said.

It was the shock, the whole thing. I shut the door on him. Watched Brandon leave from behind the curtains, then I let go of them when I saw him wrapped up in their material, his tiny face stuck to the heater. He'd been a beautiful boy.

I wiped my hands on my trousers then went and washed them. It was the shock. Until recently I've only had a nodding acquaintance with failure.

It wasn't your fault or your responsibility. It was just one of those things where my child's life was ruined, said Tanya.

It isn't ruined, Tanya. I don't know who I was trying to convince.

You know a lot about people's minds, granted, she said, but don't assume that you know a young man who you last saw when he was a four-year-old child: a frightened child who didn't know then that he was going to feel like he does now. Unemployable. Unlovable.

You love Brandon, don't you?

Well, yes! Everyone loves Brandon. Will a woman? He's at that age when his friends are dating, some are getting engaged.

Getting married isn't everything. I never did it.

Don't I know it! My marriage certificate wasn't worth writing on toilet paper.

I asked her if the children's father ever came back after the accident. He hadn't.

Archie always made messes harder to clean. He would've added his own mess on top.

You wouldn't have wanted that.

That's right. I've enough on my plate, don't I? Tanya said sarcastically. Things have been on autopilot, some things boxed away.

Mother felt bad too, the heater being on, and her leaving the children alone when she should have been watching them, while she ran her bath. Rightfully, she wouldn't have been minding them if I hadn't asked it of her. And I wouldn't have thought I could help Tanya if she hadn't seemed so helpless. If we could cast blame far enough back, I sometimes think we'd never be done.

I am not the success in your book, Graham. I'm sorry to tell you that I am no one's achievement.

I reminded Tanya that her family was still together.

We're dangling. Carla's going to London and leaving me with a business that is killing me. She doesn't know.

Children are more perceptive than you think, I told her.

Are you still analysing me?

Something will come up for Brandon. Isn't he an adult now anyway? Carla too? Perhaps you should ease off.

Tanya scoffed. Says the man who never married! Says the man who never had any family. *The theorist.*

You're wrong there, I have a son. Davis is twelve, I told her. I took no pleasure in making the correction.

And you've left him too. Twelve, you say? That's an important age, for a boy.

Every age is important for everybody, I know it for a fact, but I didn't say it.

Tanya started to laugh then. You dark horse, you! How come I didn't know any of this?

How would you? I asked her.

You have always been this enigma, haven't you? You're not really a people-person for someone so interested in others... I've always found it strange. When are you going to see Davis again?

He'll stay with me later in the holidays, if the job transpires. They are saying I don't have a degree, it's a nightmare!

What! She allowed herself an honest laugh. That's strange.

Strange things happen, Tanya, I told her. Strange people hand you a rolled-up scroll at your graduation ceremony with a printed note rolled inside that tells you to collect your certificate another time, that it's not ready. I stood as I spoke. It happens to a few of your peers too, so you get drunk and you forget about it, you get a job in the hospital and no one asks for proof of qualifications. I started to pace. You do a masters, then a doctorate and you research...you write books about mental health. Then you move away and apply for a new job, they order copies of your qualifications. You get told that you didn't complete some of the modules of your degree although all the wanking coursework is still here, and the exams all marked and scored, with distinction, in red pen. The papers, bundles and bundles of them, are stashed in the roof-space of your dead mother's decrepit gate lodge. There's nothing anyone can do. It's unfortunate, they say, you need to go back to university and get a degree. Yet you used to teach the bloody course. It's a fucking farce!

I lifted my foot to give the cardboard box a kick. Just a little one. Swung my leg back in a measured movement then thought the better of it. Put my foot back on the floor. I couldn't go about kicking things. It had been enough that I'd kicked the heater over after the call. And I'd left the heater like that for a good week or so until Tanya arrived to see it.

Christ on a bike! she exclaimed.

So I'm a fake, I said. I'm like that couch under you.

Ah, you weren't to know. It was the way she would have spoken to Carla and Brandon. A soft, reassuring tone that worked on all class of creature.

No, but I should have known, like the book I wrote about your case, that led to the other books... my ideas about psychotherapy. I have a hypnotherapy technique named after me, for God's sake. Suddenly it's just one long tail of under-achievement.

I read about the technique. Tanya blushed, she looked young again, like when we worked on the psychiatric ward together. When I'd brought her the card from the ward staff, I advised Tanya to look for work elsewhere. She didn't have the heart for the job. No, I understood she had too much heart, was what it was. Tanya weighed practically nothing and was attacked one night by a patient undergoing a pretty unethical, and not to mention sudden, withdrawal of meds. Dr Stoops hadn't been a rota man. Stoops had scheduled her to work alone.

You helped me, back then, Tanya said.

I didn't know if she meant when we were colleagues, or when she began to come to Mother's through the back door so that I could help her eat again. It's always bothered me that I don't know what people are thinking. If crime pays police and legal professionals, then irrational thoughts pay mental health workers. Sound thoughts are the map we are all trying hard not to stray from.

I'm afraid I didn't help you. Not permanently. I sat back down.

Is anything permanent? You would've had to have gone back in time to when we were kids. And how would you've done it? You could only help me now. I mean, then, said Tanya.

We talked for a while after that, me taking my cue to feel sorry for myself and Tanya insisting that I had helped her and maybe now I could help Brandon. She said something about how she used to see me out in town, enjoying myself. I took it that she was implying that I had a problem with drink when I had many problems, yet drink barely made the grade. People say, he knows how to enjoy himself, and what they really mean is, he doesn't know how to enjoy himself, he needs a drink to forget his life for a few hours. Now I don't drink a lot. Certainly not enough.

Things got stifled and uncomfortable for a while between us as we sorted and re-sorted our thoughts, disregarding the wrong things to say. Tanya eventually settled on asking me about the Provost job again: the safe ground. I told her that if it didn't come to fruition that I would go back to England. Escape into fiction. I could write stories based on what I'd learnt and change more names.

You don't happen to have a Dictaphone sitting about, Tanya joked. I'm not a recurring character. Am I?

We both need a change. You need to put some distance between you and your problems, Tanya.

At that point she looked drained. What, run away, like you? Why would you never tell me the answers before, when I used to beg you for them? Now you're full of wisdom. And your idea is: have a getaway plan! Brandon blames you... He was here, outside, earlier. He's angry, has some skewed version of events.

False memory. He was here before too, I told Tanya.

Why didn't you say? What did he say? There was panic piped around the edge of her voice.

He just wanted to see where he got burnt, I tried to sound calm, ashamed at how I'd acted when I'd seen him.

My son, my Brandon, used to talk about his stepdad. I never knew what he was on about. Now he's walking around in a body he doesn't want. He hit a girl.

I told her I'd heard.

This bloody town! He was in a bar, the girl screamed in his face, he'd had a bad day, people saying things to him on the football pitch. That's where he lives, the football pitch, used to anyway, before he hit... her. Graham, was it inevitable that we would stray? That we weren't strong enough to hold it all together?

Who do you mean?

Not you, don't worry!

No, I didn't think you meant me. Archie?

Tanya nodded.

At least he didn't bother you again, is that right?

It turns out that the moment he got a sniff of someone else he stopped *bothering* me. God knows what way he treated her, before the next mug.

That's not your problem, Tanya.

He isn't well now. Archie's suffering too, in his own way.

How does that make you feel?

How does that make me feel? That's more like the Graham I know! Archie doesn't see the kids. He's hurting more than he hurt me. It's some consolation.

It was my turn to nod. You look better, despite everything. You look good, Tanya.

Maybe that's a recent thing, she said. I've only ever looked good under your light.

A thump landed on the window. There Brandon stood, looking in. Just as suddenly as the past meets the present Tanya's face changed. She no longer looked good. She looked sadder than I'd ever seen her. It was understandable. You are only as happy as your least happy child, to use a phrase of my mother's.

FRIEND REQUEST

Dear Joan,

I hope it's not weird that I've looked at your photos, it's just that you've made them public. Social media has always felt to me like a conclusion: we can learn how lost school-friends have turned out, but needless to say, we're not walking in at the end of their story.

I was surprised to find you here, if I'm honest. You and I aren't young like your daughter Gabrielle (pretty name) or like my niece Brooklynne (remember Annmarie's daughter?), still you've signed up to showcase the parts of your life you think look enviable. Which makes me wonder what aspects of my own I'd put on display here, if I were planning to stay past this message.

Brooklynne says private messages follow their own social etiquette. And you're more computer savvy than I am. I see you've had a profile on Facebook for years but for me it was only today that I set everything out and saw what I'd long forgotten.

On your *wall* it says: Joan lives in Lincolnshire. Very nice! If I had your full address I'd write you a letter, although by the time I'd get round to posting it, I might end up tearing the thing up.

So you've never married either, that or you have and you've kept your name, which would be a very *you* thing to do. All these years and look how easy you were to find.

Imagine the trouble we'd have gotten ourselves into if there had been the internet when we were girls. Now I'm thinking about the game we played in class: you'd write a man's name, fold the page and hand it to me, then I'd jot down some puerile sexual activity. You, a woman's name. Then I, a location. Remember in physics, Mr Fisher confiscated our page and started to read it aloud? Getting as far as his own name, the word cunnilingus... Ha! He couldn't bring himself to tell our parents exactly what we had him doing in the storeroom to the dinner-lady. They never quite knew what they were punishing us for. And that's exactly how I felt, years later from you.

I haven't had children, Joan, but I read the news and I know. Predators lurk on this thing. Every day there's a headline about it. When Brooklynne first set me up with an email account she told me not to trust anything, competitions' wins could be viruses. 'Don't open that email.' And 'This one can wreck your PC.' So I didn't.

Today she found a photo. Brooklynne said to me, Look at this oldie, and she spun her laptop around — oldies are what photos from the 90s are now, like our parents listening to the Stones when we were young. God, and they're still doing the rounds! In the 90s Brooklynne was a child, Glenn was still with us and, in that respect, it does seem like a hundred years ago. You eventually managed to slip from my mind but Glenn still skulks around.

Earlier, I was thinking about what should've been our honeymoon, how I spent it with you instead. We were watching the evening entertainment on the terrace when that young couple joined our company. He was from here and she was Scottish. They were trying to suss us out the way strangers abroad do. You said you'd studied Irish dance for five years. Joan, we'd been friends since first year of Jameson High and I'd no idea.

He was chatting me up, because that's another thing that happens on holidays, people allow their partners to flirt with others, they get turned on by it or one of them ends up having to wear dark sunglasses the rest of their holiday, it's most obvious at the breakfast buffet.

The man said, I've noticed you about the poolside with no man on your arm, yet you're wearing this sparkler. He held my hand, looked at my engagement ring.

My fiancé died in a car accident a month ago, I said. Joan here, I waggled my glass at you, thought it would do me good to get away.

They praised you, as if you were doing poor old me a favour when for years it was the other way around. Later that older couple from Dublin came over. When are you getting married? they asked me. I looked at you and said, You want to tell them?

You looked affronted. No. It's not my story to tell, you said with conviction.

Back in our room you asked if I would hang the Do Not Disturb on the door, you wanted a lie-in next morning. Whatever the maid used to clean the room, you said made you feel queasy.

Months before the wedding date you said it was the Winter Solstice Sunset. That was the kind of thing you talked about, with your magenta streaks in your hair and your studded nose. We all went to the Ring of Gullion. I used to have to beg Glenn to allow you along, just so you know.

We three sat in the passage tomb, the winter sunlight swamping the stones. Me. Him. You. You picked the gloves off your fingers, I could've sworn it was to let the back of your hand touch his but I let it go, not wanting you to have no one during a sunset. I was in the communal spirit.

Who decides if a place is an area of outstanding natural beauty? Glenn asked as we walked back to the car he later died inside. You were asking him to deny that it was beautiful.

Eye of the beholder, Glenn said.

I was too tired to enter the conversation, I listened amused. I'd only wanted to spend time with both of you and feel part of something blessed, because you'd always been vocal about my boyfriends in the past. I'd ditched Rab on your recommendation, after he'd leaned over you to speak to me at a party and grazed your breast with his arm. But Glenn, you liked. You cried almost as much as I did when they brought his body back to his mum's house — remember he and I couldn't live over the brush with his religious grandparents still living. They wouldn't approve.

In Alcudia I spoke about the little semi-detached house Glenn and I had put an offer on back home, how it was on the market again. I was going to miss out on it and you'd been dying to get out of your folks' place too. But you said you were going, you would've loved us to live together but... and your eyes welled up. There were mounting mysteries, like Irish dancing and things in England that were none of my business, even though I'd told you every little detail that was mine: how Rab was so fervent and sloppy in bed compared to Glenn who was tender, and if anything had to be told to be a bit more... well, just more, and you would laugh at that, hiding your teeth with your hand because you never got a brace when you should have.

I see you've had them fixed now. Veneers? Brooklynne's a dental nurse, that's why I ask. She's big into teeth whitening. Once a month a woman comes to the dentist's where Brooklynne works to administer Botox injections. My sister — you know, Annmarie — gets poison shot into her forehead so she can't frown. People are able to make themselves into anything they want now. Whatever they don't like they just scrape away. Start again. I know, I sound disillusioned, the notion that we can change who we are from the mind down is nothing new.

When Glenn and I plotted our marital home, I asked him for a puppy. He said dogs were dumb and always got neglected once babies came along anyway. I pictured our brood. Joan, you just wanted the one, and you got her. Glenn wanted kids too but I couldn't get him to agree on the dog, though I have three now. I'm not talking about dogs, really, what I'm talking about is Glenn's indifference to nature, to sunsets and animals, and yet when Brooklynne said, Auntie, do you recognise anybody in these photos, I looked at the wildlife march walking up our streets — which are just *my* streets now, I suppose. I looked at Facebook, here is where she found them, and I said, He went to school with your mum, then, Oh, she worked in Joe Hammill's newsagents. There was that Boston Terrier that must be dead for decades by now, there was that poor skinny wee woman whose child's got burnt by the gas heater, and in the background was you, doing your bit for our planet, which, ironically, I see you don't care too much about anymore, with these snaps of you beside a huge 4x4 outside your country home. Fur coat. Sheepskin boots. All that's missing is a foxtail in your hand.

Glenn was there, in the photo—recycle-my-hole!-Glenn—his arm over your shoulder, your arm around his waist, you're looking at each other. I know those looks, because I was often there with you when you were getting off with guys, and obviously I know what lust looked like on Glenn.

You and he were in the middle of town, in front of everyone I'd grown up with. They all acted awkward around me after he died. They referred to you as 'yer woman'. I see yer woman has taken herself off to England. Best place for her type. Stupidly I thought they meant hippies.

I've been looking at Gabrielle's Twenty First Birthday photo album. Calculating. I've looked at this album more than a love letter. On holiday with you, she has her trouser legs rolled up and no socks, like he always did. Did you teach her that? Have you ever noticed Gabrielle's long slim ankles are his?

I understand why you never got in touch, but understand this, I felt like I'd been bereaved twice. I tried to contact you but all had gone quiet on the Joan-front, bar one Christmas card which neglected to tell me you'd given birth to the baby who should've been mine. No. That sounds ridiculous, but I won't scrap this message again, I may regret it tomorrow, but I regret more the silent things.

You might say this is all pointless at this stage, you've had Gabrielle twenty years longer than I had her father. You had Glenn...when? When I was working shifts? Gabrielle is more real than Glenn ever was to either of us. I know it's past news to you but it's new to me.

Nights we had sleepovers we resolved how our lives were going to turn out, peppered our visions with the things we would never do. You begged me to get rid of Rab, saying you could never go out with a boy who'd felt your friend's tit. I lay thinking that boys came and went but friends were for life and here we are, decades later, and I'm sending you a request to be my friend when really you always held me back.

Brooklynne says you may have updates that are private. And I need to see. I need to see who this new Joan is. I need to wake up tomorrow and realise I've known everything all along, so I can go back to my life and forget about you again.

Sally

THROUGH THE CRACKS

Ten years ago I was dying to meet you, Micah. I bought us matching pyjamas for the hospital. It rained so much I thought it would never end. You were as bald as a fish in the lough and met me with that brilliantine inquisitive look: the quicksilver flash from the whites of your eyes at times ensconced behind delicate purple lids.

*

She kicked our mat against the patio door, my mother — your grandmother — fresh from mass on the far corner of Belfast, heels of her hands on the hips of her summer Sunday wear, which consisted of: a linen skirt and shirt in lemon, tan suede shoes made for comfort, the crucifix around her neck swinging, glinting gold. It is these little details I remember.

    That afternoon was baked to perfection. The half raspberry stained lollipop stick, you had your father peg to your bicycle's chain-stay, tutted against the spokes: a softly frantic applaud for you for graduating from three wheels. Other noises of summer buzzed alongside the unevenness of your training wheels, bumping up and off the patio, though we discounted those extra props and only recognised the permanent pair.

Over the course of the next hour or so your father took his time, fetching Stellas from the fridge and platters of meat for searing until unrecognisable. That lackadaisical man looked serenely happy, you see, inside every man is a touch of boy, it could have been you, really.

It turned out that your auntie Dominique and her partner Eoghan were here not two minutes, after pleasantries, before they helped out: Dominique indoors, Eoghan in keeping your father convoyed and advised. And I use the term *helped* very loosely indeed. The men were going to make kebabs, they were going to go something like: pork, mushroom, pepper, then over, the length of each metal skewer. They probably would have botched them up, like every barbecue before.

Dominique had brought a shop-got meringue base, she attempted to hand-whisk the cream in our kitchen, it would only have collapsed in the heat of her car if she'd made it at home, she explained.
Listen to Delia here, would you, your grandmother said.

Apparently the muscles in Dominique's forearm were bunched and sore, so she found the electrical whisk I'd shunted, still in its box, to the back of the cupboard. After the job was done she wavered the attachment enough to attract you: like a little bee to honey, to lick away the cream. They let you help, someone lifted you onto the counter where you were given various jobs to do, then someone lifted you down. And you were gone.

A small thing like a bare-footed three-year-old boy can disappear: a small-for-his-age strawberry-blonde child, whose hair had whitened in fronds around the forehead from your recent outdoor play. You reminded me of a dandelion, and of being young myself. Micah, I was once curious about the world too: I tweezed veins from leaves, scored pink rose petals purple with jagged-edged stones, used my litmus paper tongue to test melty rainwater and the gummy spring-dew on blades of grass. I remember.

Where's Micah? your father asked like he'd done a thousand odd times before: once for every day of your life, when he would come home from painting and you would already be sleeping, or when he could see you just fine, in tireless games of peek-a-boo. Can't see him out there, he said.

Must be in his room, said Eoghan, in for a top-up of lemonade — we refrained from letting you call him *uncle* just in case Dominique dropped him, which invariably she did. Arms folded, Dominique strutted into our square lawn: a little freshly-mown playpen for a toddler. She'd been subdued, was rowing with her man and making sure he wasn't alone in feeling the discomfort. I ignore her when she's like that, she comes round eventually.

Your grandmother looked around the kitchen, under the table, in the downstairs loo, places you were renowned for hiding out.

Call him, I said, pulling apart buttermilk rolls so fresh that any additional butter was quickly eaten up by them. Your father did, he set his tongs on the kitchen counter, shouted, Micah? while outside his stack of charred burgers slumped, looked in need of their own scaffold.

Next thing I did was to pick up the bowl of strawberries and plant them into the pavlova cream, careful to use the perfect ones, popping any ones you'd cut unevenly with your little plastic knife, straight into my mouth. I heard your father upstairs, pulling your cabin-bed out to get at the cubbyhole, with little logic that you couldn't have moved that tonne of timber in the first place.

Micah? I added to the commotion, twisting the strawberry juice from my hands into my apron. The sound of door handles banging off the upstairs walls made me unpick the strings and shoot my apron straight into the sink. It is mighty how the body obeys the heart.

The creak of our ancient floorboards and the feeling, overhead, that your father was in our room — his and mine — must have made me his underwater co-ordinate, don't you think? I knew he was at the window, for when he'd slept off long enlightened hours in his studio, your little face would have illuminated to hear that creak, the rolling swipe of curtain rings: daddy was up! Why should those groaning floorboards give me such a gut-punch that something was so badly wrong? I see him! Your father burst down the stairs, exploding through the patio door like air would from a paper bag, blown under a car tyre, or perhaps he said nothing and his face was what said it. He headed for the fence and the forgotten gap.

Is he there, Sam? God bless us. My mother felt for a peekable knothole in the wood beside your father, visibly concerned by his silence. They still have a dog? she asked. Micah, darling, just stay where you are.

No... no dog, I uttered. We were the ones who had had the dog. Why had we never patched up the fence after Harvey's kidneys gave out on him? A year later and you were born. It was a long time before you could walk, and so we never imagined that you would regress back to all fours and crawl out. Harvey would have had to practically dislocate his shoulder bones to drag the rest of him behind, poker-straight legs and all, to lie on the neighbour's scutch grass and nose the frogs. The late Mrs Grier, Beth, would insist, He's fine! that our retriever, our old golden boy, kept her company when she was out making their retirement garden beautiful.

Your father cracked the fence up like a shutter, second-thought himself and clambered onto the table where Eoghan was positioning a chair in preparation to climb on to it himself, your father hauled himself over the fence, decanting the petals of Mr Grier's roses over our side. With his weight and the fence's height, it was tough. Tough to watch.

Then came the splash, your father's cry, shrill and fey. I was pulled into the grass. There I screamed.

*

For days there wasn't a speck of rain on the hospital window. I sat tousling your cow's lick, sweeping your hair back out of your face as if it had moved when you hadn't. Not an inch.

Devoid of your little spectacles there sat the flawless china of your skin without interruption. Your father paced about as if we were waiting for something fine: we were good together in times like that. He would sit for small periods and proffer an arm over mine, I had to get used to its weight, we'd lived for so long in a sense of separateness that it felt like we were coming back together: like when I'd pushed you from that other world, before it returned for you in that side-room, and claimed you back with our signed agreement and silent acceptance.

Your lips lost the true-blue lines like on a pregnancy test. Cold-chafed. An ache inside a scar in winter. Then we were allowed to take you home. Mr Grier was carried in with the swell of visitors after further days yet. I almost didn't recognise him, it had been years since he'd needed to return Harvey to us, and then I'd only ever caught a glimpse of him through the cracks. He stood on a closely balanced tightrope of regret and tenacity that it was our fence, *not* his: I could hear it in his voice among the obligatory, cursory references he coughed out of himself about *young Micah*. And his sighs, the house was full of them, full of nothing but other people's air.

Mr Grier had cut back the thick shrubby growth on the other side. He must have, because I think I'd thought you were blocked in by nature, nature deciding it wouldn't be so cruel, not to me. Not me. My eyes were drawn from where your bicycle sat straddling the fence, back to you, back home.

But back here your father and I were a crumbling edifice, his palm was chalk-dry in mine. I knew he would go: wipe off, rub away, unlike names and dates and stone — nothing is as permanent as names and dates *on* stone.

In the house I realised the walls had given only an illusion of security. Your father left to rent a room in a house like a student, we were fork-ends and dropouts again. I begged him to come home. He couldn't answer, except to say that he was feeling a bit better, given time he no longer had something weighing on his mind heavier than you had in his arms: two stone dripping wet, something immeasurable on any scale.

He'd wanted us to move together, to Lisburn maybe, somewhere close enough to Belfast's galleries but distant enough from that Sunday afternoon, it was so he wouldn't have to see the pond every morning and night like an old pair of pyjamas that once buttoned him into some dreadful sleep. And now I just don't know. It seems that there are many things I am still waiting to awaken from. I knew I'd only take it with me, I knew I didn't want to leave it — to leave you — and so I refused to go.

His first move was to our spare room. The front of the house. Your father was the creative while I was the academic, he was uninterested in *what ifs*, though never bored of slicing onions and sketching line drawings of their insides: an endless stream of layers, Russian doll-esque, featureless in his flavourless studio where he spent hours making childlike prints. It was salutary, I suppose, for him.

I swallowed those onions with my feelings. Ate every pain. My stomach skin expanding, then drooping down like a bib, concealing where you'd first sparked to existence as a physical well-sown life: my vernix-streaked idea of somehow leaving something of myself to this world. *This world?* What did I think I was doing? It was the wrong way round, fittingly breech like you: blue feet in a blue bag, slid away, feet first.

I'm sorry to say that for a time I shut out the remnants of our life as if I had turned a tap anti-clockwise, back to the comfortably remote grungy girl I was, humming along to Nirvana in my girlhood home. Your *chronically-uncreative* grandmother once went through her own artsy fad of glue-gunning dried husk flowers and peach satin ribbons to the brims of wicker hats, you know, and hanging them on to my bedroom walls. She was trying to edge Kurt Cobain out, his low sorrowful strums reverberating so deeply then that I didn't need to have lost something precious to truly know how it would feel. I resented the wall accessories. And now I tell myself that Cobain succumbed in the end, and to worse things, chocolate cannot be considered a *hard* drug.

Your father — and no longer *my* anything — never subscribed to any ABC of bereavement: he ignored the pity of friends, psychoanalysis from my sister and my mother's prayers for all of us. When he felt angry, boy, did he feel angry! For me, reading about stages and processes of emotions replaced any religion that had ever floated behind my eyes. It comes and it comes and it comes. And music, music lifted me and it floored me. And the food, I admit, is an issue.

Life was nothing like those awkward divorcee exchanges in the movies you never grew to see: and with no *you*, and mortgage banking now primarily done online, there was no reason for your father to visit. Though I did see him, once, in the window of a bistro on the Bloomfield Road, it was a couple of years back, he was huddled against a candle-dim table, his suit trousers washed out of sync with his jacket, which was still velvet-black. I almost waved out of habit then there she was: a woman he would have the blind joy of not knowing how she would handle grief, until a later date, unless he gave up on her too fast to find out, a woman who was laughing so hard she was nearly crying, jiggling her shoulders, everything.

I slung my handbag into the passenger seat and drove, sputtered through every puddle, parked beside the hardware shop. The corrugated roof shivering under the street light. That evening I landed home with a mountain of wooden slats in my arms, Mr Grier heard the clatter of them from his end.

A patch-up job is as bad as a hole, he said, the rain-soaked top of his head visible over the fence, his legs partly obscuring my view of the pond, the water catching raindrops and tossing them back. He offered to help but I brushed his offer aside and whacked the slats into place with a hammer and a mouthful of nails. Later in the week he came to the door, Mr Grier scratching behind his ear, a van behind him had the painted words *Man with a Van* almost flaked off.

Please, Annaliese, let me, he said.

Inside the van was a replacement fence panel, a wooden trough, compost and bulbs. It was a gesture too big to ignore, too small to help.

They took down the fence, Micah. Put up a new one with the trough covering the escape-spot like a tiny memorial garden for a tiny soul. Your grandmother comes to preen it, and to pester me into attending a church service with her some week. She says, There're people who always ask after you. I say, Maybe I will...some week. I insist that she leaves the dandelions be.

When they carted the rotted wood off to the van, for a few minutes I stepped into Mr Grier's parallel world. I imagined I saw you, floating starfish: face down, your little glasses gone, hair billowing something fairylike. Your fingers and toes were outstretched, waving you away.

IRL

On Monday morning Ellen took a cab to the surgery. The copy of Vogue the secretary gave her to skim while she waited didn't help her situation a whole lot. On the loop of pages on Ellen's lap was a girl, all of about sixteen years old, swinging a Lulu Guinness purse. Some stylist had crimped the child's beige hair into crenelated zigzags, to loosen the buttocky lines of her jaw. She wasn't even cute, this model, thought Ellen. Pretty didn't seem to matter anymore, just quirk and youth. Just being thin as a string bean.

On the next page was the same girl, beige hair tied-up now, a sleepy sheen glossed over her eyes like she'd just caught forty in a gold-plated four post bed. Ellen stiffened her legs and let them slacken again.

Some of this may or may not be true.

Wondering when next she'd eat, Ellen pressed the pages against her growling stomach, she texted Mari, telling her to stock up on something sweet for after. All Mari knew was what Ellen had told her: she was going in for a nip here, a tuck there. Thankfully Mari had no interest in the minutiae. The ageless alabaster-skinned secretary led Ellen to a spartan room and told her to wait there. Ellen watched the new condo towers break the skyline in Midtown Manhattan, their needle-like shadows slinking across Central Park. Ever richer, ever taller, ever thinner — it wasn't just the women. The area was becoming less *boulevard* and more gulley: a gorge lined by high stockades where no one was expected to lament the death of the boxy slabs of apartment blocks.

Ellen changed into her gown and sat back, looking out at the avenue, waiting some more. She took the photo out of her purse, the one of herself, only years before, when Masha was a just baby, Ellen looked at her own face, finding it hard to believe she had been kinda pretty and no one had had the decency to let her know.

There was a song that came over the radio, reminding Ellen of the old red barn in Arkansas: the low beams, cobwebbed ceiling, bats making sounds through their noses the way kids do when they shout down a canyon, trying to hear an echo of themselves. In his denims, Paul had strung up a hay bale, using up every inch of his ramrod back as he straightened. He had yellow hair, proper brassy yellow from Sun-In spray, he wore a shirt to match his jeans, under his popper buttons a rock band t-shirt, in the friction ridges of his fingertips dirt was permanently ingrained. Paul looked like he should never leave the 1980s.

You ain't really gonna live in NY, he told Ellen.

Last time her mother mentioned him on the phone, Paul still worked at the 7-Eleven. He turned out to have only a moiety of an idea what he was talking about. Paul never married, he had one brother, Sanford — the one Ellen eventually married. No parents to answer to.

El's Bells, I used to think of you like a sister to me, he said. Do ya think of me like a brother?

The only one I'm likely to get, she'd replied.

He laughed. I'll come visit ya in NY, he said. That's if ya go at all. You'll probably stay here. Marry Sanford and be pregnant before ya know it.

No. Not me, she said.

That's what they all say.

And I mean it. She blushed.

And I don't believe you. Paul dusted the spines of hay from his hands and walked back out, into the light. Barefoot and pregnant, he said shielding his eyes from the sun.

Ellen looked at Paul, the clouds behind him crisscrossing in the whipscarred sky. Colour rubbed off everything. It was late morning, but the way she remembered it, it was the exact midpoint of some eerie twilight, moon and sun in chorus in the sky.

I'll get this thing for your pa, Paul said. Want me to come with? Help him with this fella?

Her father had just found out from a man who knew a man, that another man, using one of his barns, wasn't sticking to the terms of rental, and was using the outhouse to cook up heroin.

Ellen nodded at Paul's offer. He went into his house. Ellen sat up front of the pickup waiting as he took an age at the back of the flatbed. When he sat beside her, she dropped the car keys. Couldn't remember ever being nimble fingered. Ellen's fingers only ever coordinated on the typewriter. Any cassette that tangled, she managed to snap the tape in the rescue mission.

Tootle over, Els, Paul said. Let me behind the wheel.

He pressed play on the tape in the deck, a power ballad played as they drove down the unpaved roads. Then the song jammed. Ellen listened to the clicks of her own jaw as she yawned. Where one particular road elbowed off to the left, they came to a stop. Her father was there, smoking his cigar outside the family home. He offered one to Paul, the two of them smoked while Ellen left them to it and headed inside.

The whole time they were gone Ellen had been in her room: first she ate the club sandwich her mother brought her, then she lost the rest of the day to a book, couldn't remember which one. She stopped reading for a good year after. It was hours later when she heard her father calling. It was twilight then. Maybe that's why it stuck.

Paul and her father had driven to the barn, they had, inside a bale, two sawn-off shotguns. The man wasn't alone when they got there. There was a fight between a bunch of them, the heroin chef took a hit to the side, an inch or two from his vital organs. Ellen's father jumped into the pickup and drove, leaving Paul to run back home through the wheat plains.

Coming up to Paul's trial, Ellen's father fell face-first into a bowl of winter salad. Ellen was pouring a honey and mustard dressing. She had a ringside seat for his death. It was a major stroke. Paul was put away for four years for being there, at the scene, before they accepted it wasn't him who pulled the trigger.

When she was under, Ellen was sure she was a goner: she dreamed she had been shot in the face, and in both sides. When she woke from surgery her face was hurting bad, she couldn't bend for the lipo compresses. Ellen felt well and truly razed. Bulldozed several times.

Mari came and collected her, she brought her cairn terrier Beano. Beano provided something to look at, out of the binocular vision of Ellen's dressings. At the Hamptons, Mari trussed Ellen up like a stuffed doll on the porch — the movie *Weekend at Bernie's* leapt to her mind — the ocean breeze cooling her pains. Mari held the glass for her as Ellen sucked fruit smoothies out of a straw. No leafy greens in her shakes though, Ellen was killed with gas as it was.

In those rutting hours Ellen couldn't sleep. Those glorious fevers, she welcomed them. Those feverish dreams, she had planned to write the fuck out of. But it was too sore to even lift an arm. She contemplated dictating, considered asking Mari to type, though it wasn't in her job description. Besides, Ellen couldn't talk for long. As a distraction, Mari asked her questions about her latest play, asked if it was it still running in Ireland, while she removed the excess packing.

Ellen could see her muffin face full-on in the mirror. Now the bandages merely enveloped her head like a frame. Yes, honey, Ellen told her. *Docker*'s coming to a wrap soon. Then it's starting next month in a two-bit Brooklyn theatre. A young Northern Irish girl, Carla something or other, is taking over as the Docker's wife. Truthfully, I think she'd play dirt on the floor if we asked her to, but she's pretty good at the Scottish accent, apparently.

Ellen never had the same success she had with *Twilight in Arkansas*. The reviews had been run-away. Four stars: *an utter delight*. Ellen had written *Twilight*, Sanford in the lounge, looking after Masha. All he knew at the time was that it was set back home. It was all he asked.

The play worked on account of what went on in the barn lent itself better to fiction.

Someone less solid was cast to play Ellen, a string bean WASP girl from Tribeca, who wouldn't have known Arkansas from Arkanoid. Ellen kept her father's lead role out of it. The man who was shot, she had killed off, did away with a name altogether.

Not surprisingly she changed Paul's name. She let him away with it as a consequence of the crime scene being contaminated. Ellen didn't have the heart to send Paul away. Besides she was a man's-girl. Always had been.

Sanford wasn't happy. On opening night he walked out of the theatre. Ellen came home to him packing his bag, and Masha's, he was taking her too, seeing he did everything for her, he yelled. It all got very personal. It was an infringement, to hear him tell it. Ellen threw her play-in-progress into the fire — it was garbage and she'd been looking for an excuse — her typewriter she fired at the tooth-achingly trendy, exposed-brick work of their *boxy slab* apartment wall. Sanford was not a falsely modest man. He wanted her to make a choice, but she'd rather start again from scratch. Really he was making the decision for her. Ellen knew she would have to let them go. And she did.

Since Masha was cut out of her, Ellen had something inside that didn't feel right. Earnest, po-faced nurses asked her for weeks about her *loss*, like they were talking about a death and not a birth. They were talking about blood: blood that smelt like it had been scooped from the earth's core. They also asked her about her *wound*. They had slit her belly like a melon. A grimacing gash that ran from hip to hip, instead of tucked away discreetly, like they told her it would be, inside Ellen's pubic hair, if she had not had it lasered away.

Masha was a needed child, no doubt about it, but then Ellen found something she needed more: it wasn't another man, it wasn't even money or success, but a blank page. All of a sudden Story was her church.

When Sanford took Masha, Ellen wrote a play about it. It was a two-starrer, mostly. *Gooseberry*, it was called. It was how she felt when the child came along, that Ellen was no longer needed. It was a story about a man: that man being Sanford. But men didn't like Gooseberry. They thought it was all about being a mother, it being written by a woman and all. There was not enough bloodshed to interest them. Little did they know! Ellen was dismayed and relieved.

Some of these feelings may or may not be feelings that people have felt from time to time.

Worry nibbled at her as the girl grew up. Ellen thought about Masha in Arkansas, Sanford taking her all those strides backwards. What was the point, she wondered, in him ever having left? It was because of Paul. Sanford had been happy to escape the small town tittle-tattle mentality that comes with attempted murder charges in an only brother.

Just after *Twilight in Arkansas* entered its sixth year, Paul showed up on her apartment CCTV. Ellen felt the colour drain from her. Funny thing was, he didn't even know that every night in England, Germany, even as far away as Australia, two actors played their parts as them, and that it had been the thing (as far as Sanford would admit, though Ellen thought that just an excuse) to fold his brother's marriage.

Told ya I'd come and stay with ya, Paul said, touching Ellen's mantel of awards as if he were a gloved forensics cop, touching up a crime scene.

Ellen needed him out of the apartment. They went for a walk to a noodle bar, sat down to eat, the billboard for her show less than a block away, the corner of it visible over his impossibly level shoulder. Paul never even noticed.

How do ya hear yourself think? he asked.

Quite easily, she said.

Go on, tell me. How do you block it all out?

What is there to block out?

The noise, for one thing.

Why would I do that when it's the noise I love most? She smiled as she analysed the rugged hemispheres of Paul's face: his moist dark eyes, his fat lips, like a fallen down figure eight, thin in the middle when he sucked the noodles into his mouth.

And how come you still haven't met someone, hey? he asked.

Maybe people say the same about you, Paul. Ever thought of that?

He was thoughtful for a moment. Helluva lot of Asians this neck of the woods, he said.

Just eat up and be thankful, Ellen told him, losing any remorse.

Turns out I have met someone.

Oh? she uttered.

I met her on the World Wide Web. We're meeting up tomorrow. She's the reason I'm here, he said wiping his mouth with a paper napkin.

That's nice. Though I bet she'll run you ragged, said Ellen. These people, she thought, who live in the back of beyond, how hard they try to type their way out of isolation. She'd been the same to a certain extent. Paul only laughed.

After they ate Ellen helped him locate a hostel, she drew her pashmina tighter around her.

El's Bells! Paul declared. Smarter with a stick of rhubarb!

Ellen was sure it was an insult, self-conscious in her costly clothes, her hair lacquered into a delicate structure. She knew, even back then, that she was becoming a caricature of herself. She knew that first you must be able to tell the truth about yourself, if you are to tell it about others. Virginia Woolf had taught her that. Paul's truth was that he still dressed like a teenager, his hair no longer lightened by Sun-In, but veined by God's grey. He was a less polished variety of Sanford, more lumbering in features and manner. The kind of man Ellen would have earned if she had not left Arkansas. If she had not used her brain and her brim-full chest of accessories.

A lot of foppery could fool a man into believing a woman was beautiful.

The men she attracted were smarter than Paul. Now that was hardly difficult! Some of them were really quite hot. Men would seek Ellen out no matter where in the world she was based. She never lied to them when she took their stories and braided in the beautiful and the melancholy. Most of these men were married, and the plight of the unnoticed middle-aged man was the most pathetic of all the stories Ellen could tell, more pathetic than that of the unnoticed middle-aged woman, because all women will have already had points in their lives of being treated invisibly.

Ellen wasn't calibrated for the stories that sonofabitch *old age* would bring her, the regret she'd feel twice over. For the first time in her life she could unravel layers of herself back and be rejuvenated underneath. Be poured back into herself.

Mari picked at the bandages around Ellen's hairline. Come on, let me have a little teeny-weeny peek, she said.

Mari's bra was a strange shape that drew her eye, the cups were like rims under her shirt, and it wasn't like she didn't have the breasts to fill them. Mari's breasts were touchingly upbeat. She was a type of 1980s beautiful, Ellen thought, like before hair extensions and chin implants became the norm. Her nose and cheeks were freckled like nutmeg grated on cappuccino. She wore silver sleepers in her ears. Up close on her cheek Mari had a beauty spot and a stray whisker under it. A semicolon! You could be damn certain she would have a full bush. Mari was the kind of woman who would have sucked her finger at Ellen and her mother, from the centre pages of her father's Playboy magazines. When they were bagging his jumble for Goodwill, they found a stack of such publications stored in a lustrous carpet of his padlocked ottoman.

For men it gets to a point when even the foppery doesn't work. It happens in their late boyhood, and again in late manhood. In between times, they encourage all the fakery a woman can manage.

Ellen was having her best sleep since the procedures, dreaming about the bandages coming off, that she would have some free do-over and be a regular Michelle Pfeiffer underneath. Or maybe she would have an extra eye, or her nose missing completely. It was all hunky-dory. What woke her was a scratching in the lock. A banging. Someone inside, downstairs.

Mari's bedroom door creaked open. Ellen met her on the landing, edged behind her, Mari's dressing gown gripped in one trembling hand. There was a creak creak creak in the dark. Mari reached for a switch and flicked on the lights. Lying on the sofa was a man, his back naked, from the height of the staircase, his curvy ass exposed. The scream Mari let out of her crashed like the surf in Ellen's ears. There was his train of discarded clothes from the door way, his socks still on. He looked over the top of the sofa. His young, handsome face.

Below his, Masha's.

Mom! Masha shouted, pulling the rug from the back of the sofa around herself. Get outta here!

Ellen laughed. It was not the reaction she thought she would have, to find her daughter underneath some strange guy in her summer house. C'mon, Mari, Ellen said in the accent she had cultivated long ago that didn't quite belong anywhere. That's my daughter right there.

Ellen retreated up the rest of stairs and climbed back to bed with some assistance from Mari. Eventually, Masha came to see her, she had her dress back on and sat on the edge of the bed, twisting her hair like twine, searching for split ends. You scared the life outta me, Masha muttered.

I scared you? Ellen asked her.

You said you were going to be in Ireland for another month. And what's all this? Masha pointed at the bandages around Ellen's face.

Nothing, Ellen sniped. A nip here, a tuck there. Who's that downstairs? With the nice ass?

That's Dewitt. Masha shook her head. How can I take you seriously... like this?

Dewitt, a German name?

Masha nodded.

The Germans love my plays, said Ellen.

Dewitt doesn't, Masha replied, inspecting her bitten fingernails. He's never even heard of you.

I expect that is the appeal, said Ellen. That and the nice ass.

Ellen was not annoyed, Masha was a pleasant surprise. If she didn't have something to hide, she would certainly have nothing to show. She was more like Ellen than Sanford. Ellen was elated that something of her had stuck.

Do you want us to leave? Masha asked.

Not when you came all this way for a dirty weekend.

It wasn't all this way, said Masha. I live in Brooklyn now. Have done since April.

You should have said.

You should have said you weren't living on the Emerald Isle anymore.

Masha stood, she leant in to peck her mother's bruise-blushed cheek.

A splash of morning came into the summer house. They all ate breakfast together. Dewitt seemed like a nice kid after all, although he couldn't meet Ellen's eye when she spoke to him. Dewitt sat with his forearms on his thighs, throwing a stick for Beano, regarding his knuckles like a man who had just lost in a fist fight.

Ellen looked out to the Atlantic, waves moving in rifts like in-breaths. She said to Mari, Let's walk that dog of yours. Give these kids some space for an hour. Will that be long enough, Mash?

Masha said, Mom, please don't write that little scene from last night into whatever you're working on, or I might have to move back home again. *Home-home*, you know?

No, you won't, honey. You're not as over-sensitive as Sanford, said Ellen, putting her hand out for Mari, who helped her up out of her seat, fetched her sun-hat and lead Ellen out and up the beach.

A dick-washed surf lesson was underway. Balance and determination was the gist of it, surfers bringing the sand with them into the ocean, bringing the water back out, trying to empty one into the other. Blond heads tinkling in the sun. The women sat under a tree looking at the young beach dudes for an hour, ranking their coffle of asses on the Dewitt-scale.

Just before the hour was up, they trod barefoot in the water then fanned their dresses to dry off. Ellen nearly forgot Beano was still there, aside from the shallow pants of him from under the tree. How happy he was to do his four-legged sprint back to the air-con.

At lunchtime they ate on the porch. Mari cooked fluke and

asparagus, the windows of the scullery blanched by the steam. Ellen felt the gas build like a tornado just from looking at the three bean salad. Masha would kill her if she just let rip.

Applying Chap Stick to her lips, Masha said, Uncle Paul's got a woman now.

Ellen almost dropped her fork on the deck, right where the wood was bruised, where the rust from the nails had bled. She wondered what kind of woman Paul's woman was. Ellen was certain she would have a full unlasered bush, never so much as trim, and that Paul just loved it that way. His woman would be called Sammi-Jo, or Joanne perhaps.

These names may or may not have been made up.

On the following Monday morning, Masha and Dewitt took his car back to Brooklyn. Ellen got her laptop out and started to write a play about the first, and certainly last, time she met Dewitt. She knew Masha had asked her not to, but Ellen hadn't promised a thing.

That night, as her fluid-filled fingers bounded off the keys, Ellen realised she was like a psychic in reverse, looking back over a life and telling it differently. A lot of it had to do with seeing. Ellen saw everything. Sometimes she felt like she could see into the future, she had looked so far into the past. So deep she had delved within herself. The retelling tied up ends and taught her a heap. Her freedom taught Ellen that she had travelled the world in search of the familiar. She was still glad of it.

She wrote a scene about a handsome young German man with white orb-like butt-cheeks, when they read the dialogue together the next evening Mari nearly ruptured something.

You are a bad woman, Mari said, creased over by her unsuppressed laughter, slapping Ellen's pillows down, easing her back into bed.

They would drive back to the city the next day for the grand unveiling. For a second, Ellen worried that she wouldn't be able to recognise herself. The feeling that followed wasn't a nice one. At first she day-dreamed about Paul, when she was still awake enough to guide her thoughts through one room to another, to find light where no light should be. She dreamed of him coming home from the 7-Eleven, wrists wet from pouring Slurpees. Ellen dreamed that he phoned home from around the corner to let his woman know to get his supper nuked nice and hot. A quick swoop around, he'd go into the driveway, walk up some steps, in through the house, shed his denim shirt. His woman would dress in a way that showed she cared, but not too much. Paul would sit down at the table to a steaming plate of food. Ellen imagined he wouldn't want to see any processing. He'd avoid the scullery like he'd avoid the delivery room — should this woman be a sticker. And not all out of eggs.

But did he say *hey honey* as he came in the door, did he take his woman in his arms, press his shape into her? Did he ever sit in the old red barn and wonder why he offered to help Ellen's father? Did he still think of her as a sister?

She hunkered down into a real peaceful slumber. That is to say, Ellen entered the kind of blissful state of someone who would be a whole new, better variety of oneself on the waking: an echo of that big *old* Arkansas girl she once was. New restful hours did spackle themselves in the cracks of her flaws. All night the waves rewrote the shoreline. And every thought in her was the right one.

ACKNOWLEDGEMENTS

I am grateful to the editors of the following journals and anthologies in which the stories in this collection first appeared, and to the competition judges who first saw something good in them: an earlier version of 'We Wake When We Wake' was first published in *Long Story, Short*; 'And Three Things Bumped' was first published in *The Lonely Crowd*; a shorter version of 'The Parent Trap' was first published in *Long Story, Short's* flash fiction anthology, *Sunset Drinking the Black Ocean*. 'Through the Cracks' was runner-up for the Michael McLaverty Award; 'I am Mahoro' was shortlisted for the Cúirt New Writing Prize for Fiction, and 'Playoffs' was shortlisted for the Fish Short Story Prize.

Thank you to: Anne Caughey, Claire Savage and Bernie McGill; The Square Circle Writers; Women Aloud NI, in particular Jane Talbot; Arts Council of Northern Ireland, in particular to Damian Smyth; Lisa Frank and John Walsh at Doire Press for their hard work and kindness; and the Creightons: Ryan, Madeleine, Jude, Jonah and Martha, for their love and support.

KELLY CREIGHTON is the author of *The Bones of It*, which was the San Diego Book Review's 2015 Novel of the Year, nominated for the Kate O'Brien Award and is currently on the Political Science degree study list in the United States. She has one poetry collection *Three Primes*, published by Lapwing Publications in 2013. She was runner-up for both the Michael McLaverty Award and the Abroad Writers' Conference Short-Short Story Award; and shortlisted for: the inaugural Seamus Heaney Award for New Writing, Cúirt New Writing Prize for Fiction and Fish Short Story Prize. Her poetry has been highly commended for the Gregory O'Donoghue Poetry Prize and for numerous other prizes. She has been awarded bursaries from Ards Arts, North Down and Ards Borough Council, the John Hewitt Society, Arts Council of Northern Ireland and Irish Writers Centre. Her work has appeared in numerous journals, such as *Litro*, *The Stinging Fly*, *Cyphers*, *the Honest Ulsterman*, *Spontaneity and Banshee Lit*. She founded and still edits *The Incubator* literary journal, which has showcased the contemporary Irish short story since 2014. A board member of Women Aloud NI and one of the co-founders of the Square Circle writers, Kelly also facilitates creative writing workshops, mentors new writers and works alongside community arts projects. She lives in Newtownards with her family. For more information visit kellycreighton.com.